Dracul's Revenge

DRACUL'S BLOOD

CAROL LYNNE
T.A. CHASE

Dracul's Revenge: Dracul's Blood
ISBN # 978-0-85715-077-6
©Copyright Carol Lynne and T.A. Chase 2010
Cover Art by April Martinez ©Copyright 2010
Interior text design by Claire Siemaszkiewicz
Total-E-Bound Publishing

DRACUL'S BLOOD

Dedication

To all those readers who supported me since I started this wonderful journey. Also, to Carol the best writing partner a person could ask for. I've enjoyed every moment. – *T.A. Chase*

To Susie, who received a rough draft of this book and has practically memorized it. Thanks for all the support. For Theresa, thanks for keeping me organized and lending an ear when I need to whine about something. Most especially, thanks to T.A. Working with you has been the best experience a writer could ask for. Thanks for never telling me something is too weird for a story. – *Carol Lynne*

Prologue

1447 A.D.

Radu took the urn of blood from his servant and passed it to the winemaker. "To breathe a word is your death," he growled.

The withered man bowed and retreated into the night.

Radu turned back to the servant he'd spent many pleasurable hours fucking. "You followed my instructions?"

"Yes, Your Majesty. The graves were abandoned by the time I arrived."

"Excellent. Vengeance is at hand." He leant down and kissed the servant. Although the boy had no hold on his heart, he had enjoyed the lad's innocence. Too bad his companion was growing older and tainted by the duties he was ordered to perform.

Radu stepped back and stared down at his young lover. "I'll have no further dealings in this matter. Once the wine is delivered to me, kill the maker and burn the vineyard. After the ceremony you will take one container to my brother with a note of congratulation. The remaining stock shall be placed in my cellar. Understood?"

"Yes, Your Majesty."

Chapter One

Present Day

Morgan Thompson ran his hands over the small wooden crate that had just been delivered. How many years had he waited to get his hands on such a valuable commodity?

He opened the crate and lifted the miniature clay cask he'd spent tens of thousands of dollars to obtain. Electricity seemed to travel from his fingertips, up his arms to his head as he rubbed his thumb over the ancient seal. Sweat formed on his brow as he struggled to calm his breathing.

"Will that be all for the day, Mr. Thompson?" his butler asked.

Morgan quickly tried to hide the precious cask from view. "Yes, Thornton."

What if he saw? What if he tells the others? He quickly looked around his study, knowing there was nowhere he could hide his precious elixir. *They're everywhere, pawing through my things night and day.* As soon as Thornton left the room, Morgan rushed to lock the door. There was only one way to make sure no one took his precious find.

Morgan crossed back to the desk and began to tear at the thick, red wax that covered the top of the container. *I'll not share my find with anyone.* He crossed to the liquor cabinet and pulled out his state-of-the-art bottle opener.

He managed to extract most of the cork, only a little remaining inside. Once the cask was open, he stared at his expensive purchase. A single sip was worth more than he paid his staff in a week. *That's why Thornton and the others want it.*

Morgan grinned as he poured the dark red liquid into a glass. Cask in hand, he carried both over to his chair beside the fireplace. He propped the cask against his cigar stand, making sure not to spill a drop. He swirled the precious wine, mesmerised by the way it clung to the sides of the glass. Although a heavy amount of sediment was evident, it was to be expected in one of the oldest wines ever found. Dark crimson in colour, blood immediately came to Morgan's mind. "Oh, but you are beautiful," he whispered.

He inhaled the bouquet, closing his eyes to isolate the individual ingredients used in the making. With his mouth watering at the thought of actually tasting it, he carefully put the crystal to his lips and allowed the smallest amount into his mouth.

Tears sprang to Morgan's eyes as he breathed out through his nose and savoured the flavours dancing on his tongue. Although bitter in taste, the thing he'd most wanted in the world had been worth every cent.

With each sip, his thirst grew. After the first glass, he greedily drank another, no longer taking his time. He heard footsteps above him and stared at the ceiling. *Thornton.*

Morgan knew his butler was just waiting for him to abandon the precious wine before slipping down the stairs to drink it himself. They were all jealous of his money. It was his life, and there was no way he was sharing what he'd scarified life and love for, with the maggots that worked for him.

The choice to abandon the glass and drink straight from the cask was the logical one. The more he drank, the louder the voices. He could hear them talking, plotting to break into his study.

Morgan knew he was on his own. He was an island of one and his home was being invaded by traitors. *Kill or be killed. Kill or be killed.* The phrase kept repeating in a loop through his mind as he continued to drink.

When the last of the wine hit his lips, Morgan shook the clay cask, needing another drop. *More. I need more.* The voices began again. This time his driver, Albert, as well as his housekeeper, Mary, were plotting against him.

Kill or be killed. He rose from the chair and walked towards the fireplace. The brass shaft of the poker seemed to glow, calling to him. Morgan ran a finger over the filigreed handle before gripping it in his hand. He lifted it from its resting place and felt the comfortable balance of weight.

Kill or be killed. Weapon in hand, Morgan opened the study door. His once peaceful home was now filled with betrayal. He knew Thornton was behind it. The fact that he'd been in Morgan's employ for almost forty years seemed to mean nothing to the stoic Brit.

As the eighteenth century grandfather clock began to toll the midnight hour, Morgan climbed the curved staircase.

Once on the second floor, Morgan turned down the servant's wing. He stopped in front of Mary's door. All was quiet, but he knew it was a trick.

Kill or be killed. Morgan continued to Thornton's room. With stealth not normally seen in a seventy-two year old man, he opened the door and entered the butler's quarters. Thanks to the moonlight shining through the window, he was able to study the aging man. How dare Thornton plot against him.

The first strike across the bridge of the nose caused Thornton to cry out. Morgan quickly shut the butler up before he could warn the others. A swift jab of the weapon to the man's throat silenced him.

Morgan watched as the blood began to spurt from the wound. He was mesmerised and turned on the small bedside lamp. In awe, Morgan fell to his knees and watched as the sweet crimson wine he'd drank earlier flowed from Thornton onto the bed.

He leant forward and sealed his mouth over the hole, sucking the wine from the host vessel. With each slurp of the intoxicating fluid, Morgan felt younger, stronger. *I need more.*

The ongoing mantra in his head changed to one word, over and over. *More.*

When the blood red wine pouring from Thornton's throat began to slow, Morgan rose to his feet. *More.*

Weapon in hand, Morgan entered the room of his housekeeper. The need was stronger than his anger at Mary for keeping the secret from him. He held the heavy poker above the woman's neck and plunged it through the flesh with all his renewed strength.

Mary's eyes popped open at the moment of impact. The gurgling sounds coming from the open throat seemed to mock him. How dare she. In a fit of rage, he began pummelling her body, using the poker as if it were a baseball bat. With each satisfying crunch, Morgan felt more powerful.

By the time he knelt to drink from the neck wound, he couldn't even recognise the bloody shape as his housekeeper. *More.*

After finishing with Mary, he started on his driver, Albert. He stood over the mutilated and drained body of the driver with a grin. His stomach began to spasm. *More.*

Poker in hand, Morgan wandered into the street needing more. He wasn't aware of the late night jogger until he was almost upon him. Morgan began to laugh as his target came within striking distance.

It didn't take long before the man lay in a pool of blood. On his hands and knees, Morgan took all that he could from the thin man. He enjoyed the surprise in the jogger's eyes at the first thwack of the brass poker. No longer was Morgan the reclusive millionaire who lived on the corner. He was a God.

O'Malley's Pub came to mind. How many people were gathered at the neighbourhood tavern? Would there be enough to satisfy his renewed hunger?

As he began walking towards the distant voices, he realised his blood-soaked clothing was weighing him down. The dripping suit jacket was shrugged from his shoulders, landing on the sidewalk with a splat. He left the thousand dollar piece of clothing where it landed and began to unbutton his shirt as he neared the voices.

They were talking about him, plotting. How many doctors had he seen, looking for the answers his aging body needed? Age wasn't welcomed in the shark-infested corporate world. *They lied to me.* All along, the answers to his problems had been all around him.

Morgan flexed his arm, feeling the renewed strength in his muscles. *More.*

By the time he reached the pub, he was nude from the waist up. He hid the poker behind his back upon entering the small establishment. The burly man, just inside the door, appeared to be full of the life-saving wine. It didn't take long to subdue him. One mighty crack to the back of the head and the guy fell from his stool.

As he plunged the poker into the man's neck, he heard shouting. Several patrons attempted to pull him off the vessel, but they were no match for his renewed vigour. Morgan sunk his teeth into the man's flesh, trying to rip the surrounding skin to get at more of the life-saving elixir.

He felt something slam into his back but refused to let go of the vessel's neck. Suddenly his lungs were unable to draw the oxygen needed to suck the wine. Finally releasing the man's flesh, he sat up and placed a hand over his chest. He felt the open wound as he began gasping for air.

No. Not when I've finally discovered the secret…

Chapter Two

The strobe affect of the police cars lights lent a disco feel to the dark as Detective Bobby Marks arrived at the scene. He stepped from his car and cursed the sick s.o.b. who'd ruined his night. He'd been looking forward to going home, popping an old Charlie Chan movie into his DVD player and vegging out on the couch until he fell asleep. Didn't look like that was going to happen now.

"What've we got, Hansen?" He approached the uniformed cop standing guard at the edge of the yellow caution tape.

The veteran police officer looked green around the gills. "We have a dead psycho and more blood than a Freddy Krueger movie."

"Who's Freddy Krueger?"

Hansen eyed him. "You've never seen any of the *Nightmare on Elm Street* movies?"

"Hell, Hansen, you know Marks doesn't watch that shit." Jablonsky, Bobby's partner, strolled up, hands stuffed in his pockets and toothpick clenched between his teeth.

"I forget. You haven't watched any movie made after nineteen-fifty." Hansen shook his head. "You've missed some good films, man."

"In your opinion. Now, are either of you going to tell me what's going on here? Or will I have to go search out the Lieutenant?"

Both men stiffened. The Lieutenant was a petite, but hard-nosed lady from Alabama who didn't put up with much from her officers. Bobby didn't have a problem with her, mostly because he did his job and didn't think that because she was a woman, she was soft. He'd seen her take down a two hundred and fifty pound man all on her own. He wasn't going to mess with her. The other officers were scared of her and she liked that.

Jablonsky lifted the tape for Bobby to duck under. "What we have here is a violent murder with several witnesses."

"Aren't all murders, by their very nature, violent?" Bobby hid his grin as his partner glared at him.

"Shut up, smart ass. What I'm saying is, this guy didn't care that O'Malley's was full of people. He didn't seem even to notice they were around. From what I've gotten so far, he walked into the pub, swung a fire poker at this big guy inside the door. Once the guy was down, he jabbed the sharp end into the guy's neck and started drinking his blood."

Bobby held up his hand to stop Jablonsky's recitation. "Drinking his blood?"

His partner of five years shuddered. "I've seen a lot of murders go down, Bobby. You know that, but this one's stranger than usual. Yeah, all the witnesses say he tore at the victim's throat and was literally sucking the blood from the man's neck."

They entered O'Malley's and Bobby got his first look at the crime scene. Sheets covered two bodies and a brass fire poker lay on the ground close to the smaller of the two mounds. The metallic scent of blood mingled with the smoke and sweat tainting the air around them. Uniformed cops gathered the patrons of the pub on the other side of the room while they questioned each one. There was one man separated from the others and another homicide detective was interviewing him.

He nodded towards the pair. "What's the story with him?"

"He's the man who shot our perp." Jablonsky gestured to the nine millimetre handgun, resting on a near-by table. "Off-duty police officer stopped by for a drink before heading home. Fired one round into the man's back, but not before the man killed the victim."

"This one will haunt him," Bobby murmured as he crouched next to the bigger lump and lifted the sheet.

While slipping on the latex gloves he kept tucked in his jacket pocket, he studied the victim.

"Pretty big guy. Be hard to kill without a fight, so the perp must have caught him by surprise. Hit him in the back of the head, knocking him off his stool?" He glanced up at Jablonsky.

The other detective nodded in the direction of a tipped-over stool. "That's what the witnesses say."

"When the guy hit the floor, the poker got jammed into his neck, opening the jugular. Do you think that was on purpose, or just a lucky hit?"

The jagged hole in the victim's neck was circled with blood, dark red and crusted. Bobby didn't disturb the wound, though he leant forward to check out the tears that looked like teeth marks in the flesh.

"I don't know, man. I was looking at it being a lucky hit, but, Bobby, this guy wasn't his first victim." Jablonsky swallowed, looking like he wanted to throw up.

"If you're going to throw up, do it outside," Bobby ordered, dropping the sheet over the burly victim and moving over to the other still form. "If this guy wasn't his first, where are the others?"

"Take a look at this guy, then I'll show you the trail."

Trail? That didn't sound promising. Moving to the second corpse, he steeled himself before lifting the sheet. It was hard at times to look at the face of a killer. Even after all the years Bobby had served as a cop, he kept expecting one of them to look like the monster they really were, but none ever did.

"Holy fuck," Bobby whispered as he revealed the face of the attacker.

"Yeah. That might be one of the reasons why no one suspected him when he first walked in here." Jablonsky nudged the brown Italian leather loafer on the right foot of the dead man.

"Morgan Thompson."

Bobby would be the first to admit he didn't pay much attention to the news or things like who was rich or not, but even he had heard of Morgan Thompson. The man was a billionaire and a recluse. It was a rare day when the older gentleman left his New York City mansion, yet there he lay, covered in blood and accused of a heinous crime.

"That isn't all his or the victim's, is it? There's way too much blood."

He pointed at Thompson's body, covered almost from head to toe in blood and gore. It had been forty minutes since the man had been shot, but the blood was still damp.

"No. It's not all his."

After dropping the sheet, Bobby stood and turned to face his lieutenant. Her usually expressionless face held a grimace of disgust as she stared down at the red-streaked sheet.

"Then who else died?"

"Detective Marks, Detective Jablonsky, come with me. The techs will process the scene, and the uniforms can finish up the preliminary interviews." She turned briskly on one toe and headed out of the pub.

Bobby and his partner kept close to the lieutenant, but Bobby's mind spun at the political minefield the case was going to be. Thompson might have been anti-social to the point of being a hermit, but he had a lot of powerful friends who were going to want answers. He scrubbed his hand over his short cut hair and sighed. Why did it have to be his and Jablonsky's turn to catch a case?

The lieutenant stopped to talk to a K-9 unit standing to the side of the crowd of policemen. The German Shepherd danced around his handler's feet, eager to do what he'd been trained to do.

"Officer Monaghan took his dog and backtracked where Thompson came from. It wasn't as hard as you would think." She tapped a dark streak on the pavement with her foot. "Thompson didn't hide."

They followed the policeman and his dog down the sidewalk, and a few blocks away, they found another group of policemen, more caution tape, and another dead body.

"Seems to be the same M.O. He attacked with the poker, knocked the victim onto the ground, and stabbed him in the neck before drinking the man's blood."

A retching sound came from an alley; Bobby looked up to see a young uniformed cop doubled over.

"Rookie," Jablonsky muttered under his breath.

Bobby nodded, sympathy for the younger man twisting his stomach into knots. He'd seen plenty of murders, some even more gruesome than these, but there seemed to be something terribly evil about what Thompson had done. Killing a person before drinking their blood or not even waiting until their heart stopped beating before sipping at their life's essence like it was the finest wine.

"We have one witness who saw Thompson attack the jogger." Waving a hand at the sobbing young woman, the lieutenant shook her head. "Poor thing will have nightmares for the rest of her life."

"This is one of those cases that will dog a person for life, Lieutenant," Bobby commented as they moved away from the second group towards a large house on the corner.

"Yeah, well, I was hoping I'd go my whole career without having one of those." Jablonsky exchanged his chewed up toothpick for a new one.

"This Thompson's house?"

The lieutenant nodded and Bobby caught sight of more cops, more crime scene technicians, and more tape.

"He started here."

There was no doubt in his mind Thompson's killing spree started in his own house. Why? It was Bobby's job to find that out since they couldn't question Thompson about his motives.

"He killed his butler, housekeeper, and chauffer. Same M.O. as the others. It looks like the chauffer was the last, and when there wasn't any blood left, he went hunting. Unfortunately, he found more victims."

She halted in the front entrance of the house. Lines of blood led up the curved staircase towards the back of the house where, Bobby assumed, the servants slept.

"This is your case, Marks and Jablonsky. Don't screw it up. I've already got the Commissioner breathing down my neck, and I'll need to be able to give him answers soon. Seems the Mayor and Thompson were close enough buddies for Thompson to donate several thousands of dollars to his campaign."

Bobby rolled his eyes. Just what he needed. When City Hall got involved, things became a political landmine. Thank God, he only had to deal with the facts. The lieutenant would have to find the polite way to tell the Commissioner and the Mayor that their friend was a nut.

"I want you in my office first thing tomorrow morning with a progress report." She stalked out of the house, heading towards the bright lights of news cameras.

"Better her than me." Jablonsky spoke Bobby's thoughts aloud.

He silently agreed and climbed the stairs. He didn't want to see the servants. As much blood as covered Thompson, he knew it wouldn't be pretty. Training kicked in along with the lessons he learned from his father.

Cop work is unpleasant, Robert. If you want to be a detective, you have to man up and do your job.

Bobby's father would know all about how gruesome being a cop could be. He was a beat officer during the nineteen-seventies when David Berkowitz terrorized the city with his Son of Sam craziness, and saw the aftermath of the attacks.

Not willing to seem a coward, even to the memory of his father, Bobby took a deep breath and headed upstairs. One of the crime scene techs waved at him from the end of the hallway.

"The attacks started here."

"How sure are you of that?"

Every piece of evidence and proof needed to be perfect in the smallest detail. He didn't want his case blown apart by sloppy police work. There was no doubt who the murderer was, but he didn't want anyone to question the motive he came up with.

"Pretty sure, but we'll have definitive answers after we take all the stuff back to the lab. The blood starts in this room. It doesn't go beyond here and it doesn't look from the pattern of splatter that he backtracked over it." The lab girl seemed sure, and since the science of murder wasn't Bobby's expertise, he decided to believe her.

Standing in the doorway, he let his gaze wander, not settling on any one item. He'd learned his brain would notice if something was out of place if he didn't force it.

"Whose room is this?"

The rustling of paper from behind informed him Jablonsky was getting notes from one of the uniformed cops.

"From what they've found in the room, it was a man named Thornton. Looks like he was Thompson's butler."

"How many of the staff lived here with the perp?"

More paper shifting.

"Three. His butler, housekeeper, and chauffer. They'd all been with him for decades. Pretty lousy retirement package."

He snorted and shook his head. "He killed Thornton first. Must have been rather quiet since the others didn't react. They were all killed in their beds, right?"

The lab girl nodded, snapping more pictures that would end up on Bobby's desk in the morning.

Shoving his hands in his pockets, he made his way to the next two rooms, not entering or touching anything. There was no doubt from the amount of blood tossed around that the victims were dead. Bobby hoped they'd all died quickly after the first hit, because lying there while your employer drank your blood would be the worst kind of torture.

"Detective Marks, we found where the fire poker came from." Someone yelled up from the first floor.

"Do you think he planned it?" Jablonsky ran his fingers over the ornate carvings on the banister as they went back downstairs.

"Do I think an older reclusive billionaire sat in his study plotting to bludgeon to death three of his employees before drinking their blood?" Bobby shot his partner a glance. "No, I don't think it was pre-meditated. I think something made the poor old fool snap, and he got it in his head that they were out to get him or he was in danger."

"You know, they say that blood is the elixir of life. In all the movies, the vampires need the blood to live. Maybe Thompson believed that as well."

"Good theory, Jablonsky, but if Thompson truly believed that, why hasn't there been even a whiff of rumour about him being a vampire?" He pushed past several people standing in the doorway of what appeared to be Thompson's study.

Jablonsky clasped his hands behind his back before wandering over to the fireplace. "How do we know there haven't been any rumours? I don't read the tabloids, and you'd pitch a fit if anyone made you read something other than the Daily Racing Form."

"Shut up, shit head."

He crouched down next to a chair where a glass and clay bottle rested on their sides. The glass had a dark red residue on the side. Glancing around, he caught the eye of one of the techs.

"You get pictures of this already?"

"Yep. You can move it."

The latex gloves made picking up anything smooth a little difficult, especially when you didn't want to smudge any prints, but he managed to get the glass upright and held it to his nose.

"Hey, maybe you should make sure it's not some kind of poison before you sniff shit." Jablonsky suggested from where he stood, holding a shovel used to remove ashes from the fireplace. "What do you think? It looks like the same set as the poker."

"I didn't drink the stuff. It smells like wine, yet there's some underlying scent that I can't place." He set the glass back down for the evidence guys to bag. "The man took the best weapon he could find in the spur of the moment. I told you, Jablonsky, he didn't plan this."

Jablonsky chuckled. "Now you're some kind of wine expert, Bobby. You haven't drunk anything other than beer since we became partners."

And not much of that, Bobby added silently. It was too easy to drown the bad images his job created for him in alcohol. Oh, he drank once in a while, yet he tried not to go overboard because it wouldn't be difficult to become a drunk.

"No. We both know I know shit about wine, but that liquid smells familiar. I just can't figure out what. It'll come to me." He stood and poked the clay bottle with the toe of his boot. "Make sure this gets bagged as well. Take some really good close up pictures of it for me. Test what's left in it. If it was poison, we'll have to see if the entire bottle was tainted or if it was put into the glass."

"What you thinking, Bobby?" Jablonsky joined him in the centre of the room.

Turning, Bobby looked everything over. "Whatever caused Thompson to wig out and kill five people is in this room. I know as surely as I know what horse is going to win the third race at Belmont this Saturday."

"On a winning streak?" Jablonsky jabbed him in the side with his bony elbow.

"Won a thousand dollars last two races I bet on. My luck's been good lately, and I don't think it'll be hard to solve this case. We just need a little time, but it'll be wrapped up neatly and the lieutenant can take credit for it when we're done."

Not a word of doubt issued from Jablonsky's mouth, though he knew his partner didn't believe him.

"We should head home and grab a couple hours of sleep. I'll meet you back at the precinct, and we'll get to work on the evidence then."

Bobby eased to one corner. "I'll stay here and supervise. You head home. How are Wendy and the girls?"

"Wendy's feeling better, but now Rebecca has the flu." Jablonsky yawned. "I was up with her when I got the call."

"Go take care of your girls. I'll stay until the scene's cleared. Don't want any screw-ups. We'll get this taken care of and all the reports written before the weekend."

"Got a big date?" His partner winced when the question slipped from his lips.

Bobby never denied being gay. First thing he told Jablonsky when they became partners. No sense in acting ashamed about something he couldn't help. He also didn't flaunt his dates or encounters. Jablonsky was a good guy, kept the gay jokes to a minimum and didn't hassle Bobby.

"Just with the horses out at the track, man." He was going through a dry spell at the moment when it came to guys. "I'll see you in the morning, and we'll work out why Thompson went vampire on us."

For all of Bobby's bold words about finding an easy motive for the brutal murders, his gut told him the case was far from over. Something bad was coming, and Bobby had a gambler's feeling he was caught in the middle of it.

Chapter Three

A folder landed with a soft splat on Bobby's desk early the next morning. He jerked and dropped his feet to the floor from where he'd propped them on the edge. Yawning, he rubbed his eyes and sat up straight. The young man standing in jeans, dress shirt, and lab coat smiled.

"Late night, Detective?"

"You could say that. I didn't get back to the precinct until about an hour ago. Ton of stuff to process from multiple crime scenes." He stretched and grimaced as the vertebra in his spine popped.

"Yeah, boss downstairs said you'd want these photographs asap, which is why I brought them up here myself, instead of mailing them to you." The guy eased a little closer to Bobby.

The tone in the lab guy's voice made Bobby glance up at him. Interest gleamed in the techie's eyes. *Ah, got it. Came up here to flirt with the gay cop. Knows I won't beat his ass for it.*

"Thanks, kid. Tell your boss I owe him a drink for getting the photos to me so quickly."

"Right. Those are actually just of the perp's study. Libby, one of the crime scene photographers, knew you would be interested in those." The tech pushed away from the desk and wandered back towards the elevator, shooting a glance over his shoulder at Bobby.

Shaking his head to the unasked question, Bobby dropped his gaze to the folder. Even if the kid was his type, he didn't date people he worked with. Things tended to get a little stressful if the relationship went south. Picking up the photos, he leant back in his chair and put his feet back up on his desk.

He twirled a pencil around in his fingers while he opened the folder and started to flip through the pictures. Thompson's study screamed 'rich'. The furniture was dark heavy wood covered in some expensive looking fabric, probably silk or something like that. He hadn't gotten a close enough look at it. Bobby snorted softly. Like he would recognise silk if it bit him on the ass.

Leather bound books sat neatly in rows on the floor-to-ceiling bookshelves and looked like no one ever touched them. The knick-knacks scattered around the room probably cost more than Bobby paid in rent. The oil painting cost more than Bobby's car, which was saying something because he owned a 1969 red and black Camaro, a classic from back when they really knew how to make muscle cars.

He came to the pictures of the wine glass and the bottle. He let his feet fall to the floor and spread the photos of the wine bottle on his desk. Digging through the pile of lab reports he'd discovered on his desk, he pulled the one out about the bottle. It was clay, country of origin unknown at the moment. Samples of the clay and of the contents had been sent to the state lab for analysis and they wouldn't be getting the results back quickly. The lab was backed up from tons of other cases and just because it was a high profile one, didn't mean shit to the techies up there.

Bobby's gut told him the bottle was important. Did wineries still put wine in clay bottles or had they all changed over to glass? He scribbled questions down in his notebook. He'd have to do some research to figure out when this bottle might have been created and, if wine had been in it, when it had been made.

"Thompson collected wine." Jablonsky flopped into the chair at the desk butted up against Bobby's.

"Who did you talk to?" Bobby jotted that note down next to his questions.

"The lieutenant had me stop and talk to the other members of Thompson's staff. Seems only the three senior staff members lived at the house. The others went home every night. There's two more that we'll need to question, but that can wait for later." Jablonsky shrugged out of his jacket, rolled up the sleeves of his shirt and slid a pair of glasses on.

"Thompson collected wine, explains the bottle and glass, I guess." He traced the outline of the bottle.

"Yeah, the footman said that Thompson had attended a private auction the other night and spent a helluva lot of money on some wine. The guy didn't know anything more except that Thompson was 'stoked' about getting his hands on it. It was delivered last night."

"Explains the box on the guy's desk." Bobby let his head fall back as he stared at the ceiling. "What makes this wine so special?"

Jablonsky's chair creaked as his partner settled into it. "Don't know. Guess I should do a little investigating at the auction houses to figure out where it sold."

"Good idea. I want to know who sold it and where it came from." He looked at Jablonsky. "The wine is the key to the whole thing."

"Your gut telling you this?"

Bobby nodded. "Yeah."

He went back to inspecting the photographs of the wine bottle. "Do you think there's a special reason why the bottom of the bottle is pointed or did they make them that way whenever the wine was bottled?"

"Don't look at me. Maybe you should pick up a history on wine-making on your way home, or you could just look it up on line." Jablonsky chuckled at Bobby's scowl. "You're such a throw-back, Bobby. I don't know anyone who likes using a computer less than you."

He flipped Jablonsky the bird while his attention was drawn to the red seal on the bottle. Shifting through the pictures, he realised there wasn't a close-up, detailed photo of it. He picked up his phone and called the crime lab.

"Wilmont," the man who answer barked.

"Wilmont, this's Detective Marks."

An aggravated sigh echoed over the line. "What can I help you with, Marks?"

"I need one of your techs to take several very close shots of the seal on a clay bottle."

"The one that came from the Thompson crime scene?"

Papers being rustled reached Bobby's ear.

"Yeah."

"I'll have Libby do it and email them to you asap."

"Thanks, Wilmont. I owe you."

"Buy me a beer at the bar some night and I'll call it even." Wilmont hung up.

That would mean Bobby had to go to the bar, which he didn't do very often, but he'd make a special effort to stop at some point in the next week or two. He always paid his debts.

"I'm going to interview some of the witnesses. See if I can shake some new memories free." Jablonsky pushed to his feet, tugging on his jacket before he stepped away from the desk.

"You need me to go with you?"

"Nah. I'll take the rookie with me. She needs some practice questioning witnesses. You stay on the bottle, especially if your gut's telling you that's the key to this whole fucked-up mess."

"Catch up with you later." He waved a vague hand in Jablonsky's direction.

While Bobby waited for the lab to send him the new photos, he memorised the pictures he had. Nothing besides the bottle and glass seemed out of place or moved. That's why Bobby's mind wouldn't let go of the wine, but what could have been in the liquid that caused a relatively normal man to go crazy and brutally murder five people, then drink their blood? He wasn't sure he wanted to know.

His computer beeped and he brought up his email programme. Clicking on the attachment icon, he fidgeted while the pictures downloaded and began popping up on his screen. God, he loved digital photos. They were so clear, it was almost like the bottle was sitting right in front of him.

"Hmmm…what does that say?" he muttered, zooming in on the red seal at the neck of the bottle.

'Havasalföld' was the only words he could find on the entire clay surface. Definitely a foreign wine, or at least the bottle was. Opening his web browser, he grumbled as he typed in the word and hit enter. He printed out the new photos to add to the pile in his folder.

His old computer was taking its own sweet time finding anything on the word, so he went back to studying the seal. None of it made any sense to him. Bobby might have to call in some expert help on that. The detectives had a list of experts they could call on if they couldn't find the information on their own.

He looked up as his screen flashed. A grimace crossed his face when he saw all the foreign language links. God, he would be here all day. Couldn't one English person have translated some of these sites for uneducated people like him who could barely speak English without messing up?

"Havasalföld is a Hungarian word used to describe Wallachia, a historical and geographical area of Romania," he read aloud. "Guess that means the bottle is old."

Bobby tried to decipher more of the information on the sites, but it wasn't working for him. He scrubbed his hand over his hair in frustration before giving up and calling Cecelia, the civilian receptionist for their precinct.

"Yes?"

He smiled at the abrupt tone in her voice. "Hey Cecelia, it's Bobby."

"What can I do for you today, Detective Marks?"

Someone must be having a bad day. Of course, she was probably fielding a ton of calls from local and national media. Cecelia didn't have a lot of patience for reporters.

"I was wondering if you know someone at New York University who could help me with the case I'm working on."

Keys clicking filled the air for a moment as she brought up the contact list for NYU. "What kind of information are you looking for?"

"Someone who can help me with Romanian history." He poked at the papers on his desk, listening as Cecelia hummed softly in his ear.

"Romanian history, huh? Well, I don't have anyone listed specifically for that, but there is a Professor Nikolay Radin whose area is Eastern European history. Will that work?"

"If it doesn't, he should be able to point me in the right direction to find someone who will." He scribbled down the professor's number. "Thanks, Cecelia."

"You're welcome, Detective Marks. I hope you figure out the motive on this case. I'm tired of the phone calls already."

"I'm doing my best, sweetheart." He hung up, paused for a second to collect his thoughts and grabbed an outside line.

Bobby dialled the professor's number and drummed his fingers on his desk as he waited for someone to answer.

"History Department. How may I help you?"

"I need to speak to Professor Nikolay Radin, please. This is Detective Robert Marks of the New York Police Department."

A brief moment of surprised silence, then the female voice spoke again. "Professor Radin is in class right now. Can I get your number and have him call you when he gets back to his office?"

"How long will that be?" Bobby didn't want to wait all day, though he could research the auction where Thompson bought the wine.

"His office hours are from eleven to one, so he should be returning here in about an hour."

Bobby's stomach rumbled. "Okay, here's my cell number. Have him call me as soon as he gets in. It's about a case I'm working on and very important that I talk to him." He rattled off his number.

"Okay, Detective Marks. I'll be sure to give this to Professor Radin myself."

"Thanks."

Hanging up, he exhaled and stood. He made his way to the lieutenant's office, tapping on her door when he got there.

"Come in."

Coming to a halt in front of her desk, Bobby clasped his hands behind his back and waited until she looked at him before speaking.

"All the evidence has been catalogued and sent to the crime lab. I've got the photos from the scenes. I've started looking over them, but I'm focusing on the bottle found in the study. I think that might be our best chance at figuring out how this happened."

"Good. What's Jablonsky doing?" She jotted something down on the pad in front of her.

"He's going back and interviewing some of the witnesses. Wants to see if he gets anything new from them. Then he'll start on the auction houses in the area. We know Thompson bought some wine a couple of days earlier."

"It might be the same bottle we found at the site." The lieutenant pursed her lips and eyed him. "What are you doing now?"

"I'm heading home to grab a shower, change my clothes, and get something to eat. I have a call into Professor Nikolay Radin at NYU. He's an expert in Eastern European history, and I think the wine bottle, at least, came from Romania, very early Romania."

Nodding, she let her gaze trail over him, making him want to tug at the bottom of his jacket to get the wrinkles out. "Good idea. You're looking a little ragged. Let me know what you learn from the professor."

Bobby knew a dismissal when he heard one. He exited, pausing long enough at his desk to grab the files on the case before heading out of the building. He was looking forward to a hot shower and warm food. Maybe by the time he finished cleaning up, the professor would have called him.

* * * *

Nik gathered his papers and fled towards the safety of his office. One of his students had given him the 'I'm yours for the asking' look all through class. The last thing Nik felt like doing was turning down another date from a student. He hated the dejected expressions of the men after he informed them he didn't date students.

Entering the department's inner sanctum, Nik sighed in relief.

"Tough class?" Sheila asked.

Nik shook his head. "Student." He reached up and removed the curls that had managed to flop their way into his eyes. *I really need a haircut.*

Sheila held out several pink slips of paper. "Here are your messages. I'd look at the top one first. It's from a detective."

Confused, Nik took the papers. "Did he say what he wanted?"

"Nope."

Nik shuffled into his office and kicked the door shut without taking his gaze from the phone message. He dropped his class papers onto the corner of his desk and sat down. What on earth would a detective want to speak with him about?

Perhaps one of the many students he'd turned down had filed some kind of bogus claim against him? No, that couldn't be it. If that were the case, the Dean of Students would've contacted him first.

Nik knew he could either continue to worry about it, or he could just make the damn call and find out.

He started to lift the handset on his desk, but quickly replaced it. Maybe it would be better to call from his cell? At least he could be assured there would be no one listening in.

Shaking his head, Nik snorted his amusement at himself. One message from a detective and he was acting paranoid. He hadn't done anything wrong. Hell, he'd never done anything wrong. It was the main reason he was alone every night.

He picked the desk phone back up and punched in the number the detective had left.

"Marks," a deep, gravelly voice answered.

Nik readjusted his glasses as the effects of the voice travelled up and down his spine. "Yes, this is Professor Nikolay Radin. I had a message to call you?"

"Professor Radin, thanks for calling me back. I was wondering if you'd have time this afternoon to take a look at a few pictures? I've got a wine bottle I'm trying to find out some more information on."

"Ummm, I'd love to help you, Detective Marks, but I know very little about wine."

"It's not the wine I need help with, it's the bottle I have questions about. There's a dark red blob of wax on the bottle. From the little I've managed to dig up online, I'd guess the bottle comes from the Romanian region. It's old, real old. There's one word on the label, Havasalföld."

Nik's heart skipped a beat. "You say it's a bottle?" he asked, trying to pin down a timeframe.

"I guess, although it's not made of glass."

"Clay," Nik added for the detective.

"Yes."

"Can you bring it to me?"

"Not right now. It's at the lab being analyzed. I've got pretty detailed photographs, though. I can bring them by your office if you'd like?"

Nik almost jumped for joy. "Yes. I'd like that very much. I'm free the rest of the afternoon."

"I'm only about thirty minutes away, so I'll see ya in a few."

Nik hung up and swivelled his chair to stare at the bookshelf behind his desk. His first instincts were the bottle wasn't a bottle at all, but rather a cask. That didn't make sense though. Clay casks were large. There would be no way the detective would mistakenly call a cask a bottle. What the hell were they dealing with?

He rubbed his hands together, scanning the titles of his reference books, before pulling a particularly old one from the shelf. The pages smelled musty, the scent tickling his nose, but he knew the information was accurate.

By the time the knock on his door came, Nik had found what he'd been looking for. "Come in," he called, setting the book on the desk.

He wasn't expecting the large man that walked into his office. He should've suspected as much by the sound of the detective's voice, but the man who stood in front of his desk seemed to fill the entire office.

Nik wiped his hands on his Dockers and stood. He held out a hand and smiled. "Detective Marks?"

Marks nodded and shook Nik's hand. "You must be Professor Radin."

"That's what it says on the door." As soon as the words had left his mouth, Nik wanted to pull them back. "I'm sorry. I didn't mean that the way it sounded. Please, call me Nik."

"Okay, Nik, you can call me Bobby."

Nik gestured to a chair. "Please, have a seat."

Bobby sat and tossed a folder in front of Nik. "Those are the close-ups of the bottle and label. Any information you could give me would be appreciated."

Before opening the file, Nik took off his glasses and cleaned them on the bottom of his untucked, light-blue dress shirt. He settled them back onto his nose and opened the manila folder.

He studied the picture for a few moments before addressing the detective. "Before I begin, I'd like you to do something for me. Would you please call your lab and ask them to be extremely careful with this object. It should be in a museum, not a lab."

Bobby pulled out his phone and placed the call. "Wilmont. Yeah, I know, but I've got another favour. Tell the techs to be careful with the bottle. It sounds like it's pretty valuable. Yeah, I know. Okay, I'll catch you at the end of the week."

Bobby hung up and grinned. "I owe him another drink."

Nik had no idea what the detective was talking about, so he returned his attention back to the photographs. "Did you actually see this for yourself?"

Bobby nodded. "Yeah. Why?"

"I need to know how big it is. I can't tell from the photographs." Nik's fingernail found its way to the tortured skin of his thumb. He began picking at the self-inflicted sore as he waited for Bobby to describe the cask. He hadn't lied when he told the detective it belonged in a museum.

Bobby held his large, square hands about fourteen inches apart. "It's about this long, thin. I didn't actually hold it, but I'm sure I could've easily wrapped my hands around it.

Nik couldn't help but smile. He had no doubt the bigger man could wrap his fingers around just about anything he tried. Nik held up his much smaller hands. "What about mine? Could I wrap mine around the thickest part?"

Bobby took Nik's hands and moved them into an approximate position. "Yeah, I'd say so."

The feel of the detective's rough hands on Nik's was electrifying. Afraid of making a fool of himself, Nik pulled away and returned his attention to the book in front of him. He spun it around to face Bobby. "It sounds like you've found a smaller version of the cask in the picture. It was used to hold wine and other liquids until glass bottles began to take their place in the late fifteenth, early sixteenth century."

He glanced up and met the dark hazel eyes of the detective. Nik licked his lips, suddenly feeling parched. "Your cask was almost certainly custom made. For what reason, I'm not sure. It wouldn't have been cost effective for the wine producer."

Bobby's eyes broke contact and his attention went once again to the book in front of him. "So this cask, or whatever it's called, is really, really old."

Nik couldn't help but chuckle. "You could say that. I would probably date it mid fifteenth century, but it's hard to tell without actually examining it in person."

Please, please ask me to examine it.

"Is that something you know how to do? Date things like that?"

"Yes. Well, I could at least give you a much clearer picture of the date. Do you mind my asking where you found this particular cask?"

"It's from a case I'm working. I really can't go into details." Bobby tapped a blunt fingertip to the photograph of the wax seal. "What about that?"

Nik opened his desk drawer and pulled out a magnifying glass his dad had given him for his tenth birthday. He examined the image of the label and shook his head. "Well, you already know what the word Havasalföld refers to, but it looks like there's something else under the seal.

Nik set the magnifying glass on the desk and regarded Bobby. "Is there any way I can inspect this cask in person?"

The detective readjusted his position in the chair. "I guess I could ask. But first you have to tell me what you're hoping to find."

"The actual label is hidden under the seal. It won't be in a language your technical personnel are likely to know. I've handled artefacts; I know the proper way to remove the seal to keep intact what's hidden underneath, *and* I can translate the label itself."

Bobby scratched at his square jaw line for several moments. "I'll see what I can do."

With the weekend a heartbeat away, Nik quickly scribbled his home phone number on the manila folder before handing it back to the detective. "Just in case I get lucky, and you have something for me before Monday."

Bobby made a gruff sound in his throat and stood. He tapped the file against his thigh and stared at Nik for a moment before turning and walking out the door.

It wasn't until Nik thought about what he'd said, that he became embarrassed. *Shit.* He was always doing things like that. His foot seemed to have a permanent place in his mouth when it came to talking to good-looking men.

After the embarrassment passed, Nik grinned. Although he hadn't meant the statement the way he knew it sounded, he had to admit he wouldn't be disappointed if the detective called him for reasons other than the cask.

He reached for his book and carefully put it back on the shelf before gathering the papers he needed to grade over the weekend. If he hurried, he'd have time to run by the university library and still make his bus.

* * * *

As it turned out, catching his bus hadn't been a problem. It was getting off at the right stop that had caused him trouble. Nik had been so deep into the book he was reading, he rode almost nine blocks out of the way before realising he'd screwed up.

Instead of catching a bus back to his regular stop, he chose to walk. He had a lot of things to think about, the hunky detective being one of them. Why hadn't he just asked the guy out?

Nik had never tried to hide his sexuality. He'd been told on more than one occasion he set off anyone and everyone's gaydar the moment he opened his mouth. It was something that had never bothered him. He was who he was.

There was no doubt in Nik's mind the detective was gay, or at least bi, because he hadn't seemed uncomfortable around Nik the way most straight men were. He hadn't caught Bobby giving him any looks of lust, but he hadn't received any sneers of disgust, either.

He was almost home before he realised the books in his arms were starting to get heavy. He went to put them into his backpack and stopped in his tracks. *Damn.* Where had he left his pack? A picture of it sitting on the floor in the reference section of the library came to mind.

Nik started to pull out his phone to call the library and again cursed himself. It was in his pack along with his house keys and the papers he needed to grade. As he stood on the corner, two blocks from his apartment, he was sorely tempted to hail a cab.

With a shake of his head, he headed towards the bus stop. No sense in wasting money. He accepted the fact it would take him another two hours at least to get home and enjoy his evening. What else could he do? It was his own fault and he knew it.

As he neared the stop, he saw the bus coming around the corner. With the library books held tightly against his chest, Nik ran as fast as he could to catch it. With a swipe of his pass, he climbed aboard and looked around for an available seat. He groaned when he realised the bus was full. *Serves me right.*

Chapter Four

Drawing in a deep breath, Bobby raised his hand and knocked on the lieutenant's door. He wasn't sure how she'd react to his request, but it couldn't hurt to ask.

"Come in."

He pushed open the door and stepped in, stopping in front of her desk. She eyed him while whoever was on the other end of the phone talked to her.

"I understand, Mayor, but you have to give my men more than a day to figure out the motive. I put my best detectives on it, and I trust that they'll solve it quickly." She pinned Bobby with a glare when he coughed to cover up his snicker. "Yes, sir, I'll call you as soon as I have any information."

Bobby reminded himself he was an adult man and shouldn't run like a scared girl when the lieutenant set the receiver back in its cradle gently. Her knuckles went white where she gripped her pen.

"Tell me you have some news, and preferably it's good."

Rocking back on his heels, he shrugged. "I'm not sure how good it is, but that professor I talked to yesterday tells me the bottle found at the main crime scene is old."

"Old? I could have told you that." She snorted. "How old?"

"Like fifteenth century old. The professor says it was probably custom made, because the wine makers used larger versions of the cask." He pulled out his notebook where he'd jotted down all the things he could remember Nik saying and flipped through the pages. "It is from Romania, or whatever they called Romania back then. He thinks there's something under the seal on the bottle, some words that we wouldn't be able to read, but he could. At least that's what he says."

"Thanks for the report. Is there something else you want?"

"Yes, ma'am. I'd like you to sign off on letting the professor look at the bottle."

The lieutenant's narrow-eyed gaze made Bobby want to check if his fly was open. Standing in front of her was worse than dealing with the nuns at Catholic school. Bobby had spent a lot of time in the Mother Superior's office when he was younger.

"Why would I want to do that?"

"Like I said, Professor Radin believes there's something under the seal. He's handled objects like this bottle before and says he knows what he's doing. I guess the bottle should be in a museum and if he can find out what's under the seal without destroying the bottle, why not let him do it?"

She tapped the end of her pen against the desk while she thought about it. Bobby kept his mouth shut. No sense in pushing her. Whatever she decided, he would have to go along with. He might bend the rules a little, but he wouldn't go behind his lieutenant's back and risk losing his job or making her mad at him.

"Fine. He can come and look at the bottle, but it can't leave the lab, so make sure Wilmont is aware of the professor's visit."

"Thank you, ma'am." Bobby left her office before she could change her mind.

After returning to his desk, he picked up the phone and called the lab.

"Yes?"

"Wilmont, don't you ever go home?" He chuckled at the crude sound the head of the crime lab made. "I know all about it, man. I was hoping to get out to Belmont today for some of the races. Instead, I'm stuck at my desk because of this case."

"You shouldn't be betting on horses anyway, Marks. Not a healthy addiction." Wilmont sounded tired.

"Is there any such thing as a healthy addiction?" He hurried on before Wilmont could respond. "Can you set up a room for me down in the lab?"

"Why? When did you get your degree in forensics?" Suspicion coloured Wilmont's words.

"I have an expert coming in to look at the clay bottle we found at the main Thompson crime scene. He wants to see the bottle up close and personal. I can't take it out of the lab, so I'm bringing him to it." He shuffled some papers around, trying to find Nik's phone number.

"He knows what he's doing?"

"I don't know. He says he's handled items like this before and knows how to be careful. I don't have a lot of choice in the matter. Professor Radin is the only expert I could find and the lieutenant's getting a lot of pressure to close this case quickly. I'd like to take advantage of the professor while I have his interest."

An image of Nik popped into Bobby's head, and his cock made the rather coarse observation that it would love to take advantage of the pretty professor. He pushed that thought to the back of his mind. First things first, he had to get the case closed, then maybe he'd look into convincing Nik to go on a date with him.

Oh, he didn't need gaydar or anything like that to know the professor played on his side of the fence, though maybe he did have that mythical radar because Bobby rarely was attracted to straight men. From the moment he first saw Nik, he wanted to ask the guy out. All that unruly dark hair and those dark green eyes hidden by the wire-rimmed glasses had thrown Bobby for a second when he'd entered Nik's office. He'd thought he'd walked into the wrong place and Nik was a student. Of course, Nik didn't dress like any professor Bobby had met before either. Rumpled khakis, untucked dress shirt, and running shoes seemed more the uniform of the college kids than a professor.

"Hey, Marks, you still there?"

Blinking, he realised he'd zoned out while Wilmont was talking. "Yeah. I'm still here. Sorry, got thinking about something."

"I said bring him by. I'll set you up a spot where he can examine the bottle. The lieutenant signed off on it, didn't she?"

Bobby laughed silently. Hell, even the tech guys were afraid of her. "Yes, she did. I wouldn't have asked if she hadn't."

"Good. I'll leave a note, letting my assistant know you're coming. I'm heading home to watch some football and hang out with my kids for a while."

"Have fun, and thanks. I appreciate it."

"No problem. I want this solved as soon as you do. One less case on my plate would make me fucking thrilled."

He hung up after the dial tone told him Wilmont had ended the conversation. Nik's number jumped off the folder he'd written it on, and Bobby dialled it from his cell phone as he left the homicide unit.

"Hello?"

The soft voice answering the phone tripped over Bobby's body and goose bumps rose on his skin. What the hell was that? He'd never had that kind of reaction to anyone's voice before.

"Hello?" A slight quiver entered the voice.

"Oh, sorry about that. I got distracted, Professor Radin. This is Detective Bobby Marks. We talked yesterday."

A hitch in the breathing coming over the phone and Bobby's thoughts went in a direction they shouldn't have. What would Nik sound like while Bobby made love to him?

"I remember you, Detective Marks. How may I help you?"

"You got lucky, Nik."

Nik coughed. "What?"

Bobby pushed open the door to the car pool area and chuckled. "I said you got lucky. My lieutenant gave her permission to have you look at the bottle."

"Cask."

"Huh?" He tugged his keys out of his pocket and unlocked the sedan the department assigned him when he was on duty.

"It's not a bottle. It's a cask."

Sliding behind the wheel, he thought for a moment. "Oh right. Not a bottle, a cask. I'll try to remember that."

"When can I look at it?" The eagerness in Nik's voice brought a smile to Bobby's face.

"I'm in the car. If you give me directions to your place, and are free, I'll come get you right now."

A silent pause, like Nik had to think about it, filled the air.

"If you don't have time today, I can come on Monday and bring you back to the lab."

"No!" Nik's strident protest surprised Bobby. "I'll be ready. I'm not doing anything except grading papers anyway. Do you have a pen for the directions? I live all the way in Chelsea."

"Better than a pen, Professor. I have a GPS. Just give me your address, and I'll find my way to your place."

Bobby didn't like a lot of technology, but even he admitted that having a GPS made driving easier.

"Okay." Nik rattled off his address while Bobby typed it into the device.

"Says I'll be there in forty minutes. That give you enough time to get ready?" Bobby started the car.

"Forty minutes is fine. I'll bring some books that I think might help."

"Why am I not surprised?" he muttered, checking over his shoulder before he pulled out of his parking spot.

"What do you mean by that?" There was an edge to Nik's voice now.

"Nothing bad. You just strike me as a guy who has a book for every occasion, you know. That's not a bad thing though. It's helpful to a guy like me who had to get punished by nuns before he cracked a book."

Bobby slid into New York traffic without a problem. He hated the bland uniformity of the department cars. The sedans were plain beige, with only the police modifications done to them to make them exciting.

"Nuns?"

Not much of a conversationalist. Bobby didn't have a problem talking to anyone, which made him a good cop.

"Yeah. I went to Catholic school until my senior year, then my parents moved from Queens to Long Island. Ended up at a public school for my last year. I couldn't wait to graduate. Didn't have a clue what I was going to do, though I figured I'd end up on the police force like my old man."

Rustling came over the phone and Bobby wondered if Nik was getting dressed. *Damn.* He really needed to keep his mind out of the gutter, at least until the case was over, or he'd never get anything done.

"Your father was a policeman?"

He grinned at the thought of his pop. "A thirty year veteran of the force. Seen some nasty shit happen, but never let it get to him."

"That's good, right?"

"It is good, considering a lot of cops let the job eat them alive. They become drunks or druggies. Depression's a big job risk, along with divorce."

Bobby turned at the corner the GPS told him and continued down the street. Reluctance to end the call hampered him, but he knew he needed to let Nik get ready.

"Hey, I'm hitting some traffic, and I should let you go get your stuff together."

"Stuff? Oh, right, my books. I'll see you in a little while, Bobby."

"See ya, Nik."

After snapping his phone shut, he tossed it on the seat next to him and had a discussion with himself as he drove.

"You know you shouldn't be thinking about the professor that way. He's helping you out with a case and until it's solved, you can't cross that line."

He pursed his lips. Really, that rule applied to witnesses and suspects in cases. It was possible it didn't apply to experts called in to help with said cases.

Why couldn't Nik be some stodgy old tweed-wearing professor instead of the gorgeous bookworm he was? The man was probably older than he looked, but those glasses and clothes lent him an air of innocence that flipped all of Bobby's switches. Hell, who knew he went for innocent?

Bobby admitted to himself he liked young and pretty. That flavour was the kind he brought home from the bars when he went looking for a quick lay. Innocence, not so much. Being a cop jaded a man, and people who didn't understand the seamier side of life tended to bore Bobby fast.

Nikolay Radin projected an air of naivety and purity that usually turned Bobby off, yet there was something else about the professor teasing Bobby's interest.

"This isn't the time to think about it, Bobby, old man," he muttered. "You have a case to close and eight other murder cases you have to work on. A gorgeous college professor is totally beyond you anyway."

He wasn't the kind of guy who worried things to death, so he pushed his thoughts away. Live and let live was his motto. If something was supposed to happen between him and Nik, he'd let it. If not, then he'd treat Nik like every other expert he'd worked with in the past.

Forty minutes later, he pulled up in front of Nik's townhouse. He whistled at the expensive neighbourhood. Evidently professors' made a heck of a lot more than he thought. Before he could even get out of the car, the professor jogged down the front steps and went in front of the vehicle to get to the passenger door. When Nik was seated and buckled in, Bobby pulled away from the kerb.

"Can't wait to get your hands on my cask, huh?" he joked.

Nik ducked his head and blushed. The fall of dark curls blocked Bobby's view of Nik's face. He reached out and patted the man's knee.

"I'm just kidding, though I know you're excited about seeing the cask."

"It's a unique specimen. I've never seen one like it before." Nik's face lit up and he glanced at Bobby. "I hope we can figure out who might have commissioned it."

"Can you do that from looking at it?" He merged into traffic.

Nik shrugged, his slender shoulders moving under a wrinkled, dark red dress shirt. "It's possible, or it'll give me hints on where to look."

Bobby's stomach rumbled, reminding him he'd missed breakfast. "You want to grab some lunch before we head back to the precinct?"

* * * *

Nik emptied another packet of sugar into his iced tea and picked up his spoon. As he started to stir his drink, he noticed Bobby staring at him. "Is something wrong?"

Bobby gestured to Nik's glass. "Ya like a little tea with your sugar, do you?"

Nik grinned and sipped at his drink. "I have a bit of a sweet tooth."

"I can see that."

Nik felt his face flush. "My parents didn't allow sweets or television in the house. They thought…"

Nik shut up before he made a fool of himself. He barely knew Bobby, no sense telling him his faults upfront.

"They thought what?" Bobby rested his arms on the table and leant forward like he really was interested in hearing what Nik had to say.

Nik shrugged. "I have a tendency to be a bit…scatterbrained. My parents thought it was the sugar in my diet and too much outside stimuli. So, no candy, no TV."

He glanced up to see a big grin on Bobby's face. "I bet you're making up for lost time."

Nik grinned back. "With the candy, but I still don't own a television."

Bobby shook his head. "I thought everyone owned at least one."

Nik started to reach for another packet of sugar. He knew his tea didn't need anymore, but for some reason the detective made him antsy. On the car ride over, he'd managed to steal several glances at Bobby's powerful body. Nik wouldn't say the guy resembled a bodybuilder, but the detective sure did have his share of muscles. He reminded Nik of the men who used to work with his father on the docks.

The waitress delivered their food and Nik's jaw dropped. "They sure do give you big portions. I won't need to buy another meal the rest of the weekend."

Bobby narrowed his eyes. "Two slices of meatloaf, mashed potatoes and green beans is enough to last you a weekend?" He shook his head. "No wonder you're so tiny."

For some reason, the remark cut Nik deep. How many times, growing up, had he run home to get away from bullies who tried to pick on him for his small stature?

"Hey, I'm sorry. I was just teasin'."

Nik glanced up and saw the concern in Bobby's big hazel eyes. "It's okay. I'm used to it."

Bobby started to reach across the table but pulled his hand back before it reached Nik's. "Being small isn't necessarily a bad thing. Think of all the things you can do that I can't."

Nik snorted. "Yeah? Like what?"

Bobby appeared to be searching for examples. "Well, you can rescue kittens from drainpipes."

Nik laughed. "Yes, because there's a real need for kitten rescuers."

Bobby shrugged. "You could easily be swept off your feet and carried to bed. Can you see someone trying to do that to me?"

Nik tried to think of the last time he'd even had a lover, let alone one who'd tried to sweep him off his feet. "I had a boyfriend in college who pushed me onto the bed several times. Does that count?"

Bobby's nostrils flared briefly before he took a bite of his chicken fried steak. "No. You deserved to be carried, not pushed."

"It wasn't a mean push." Nik couldn't believe he'd just defended his ex. On second thoughts, maybe it had been a mean push. James liked to exert his power over Nik. It was what had ended up breaking them apart.

At only five-six, Nik may be small, but he was no weakling, and he'd hated when James tried to treat him like one. So why did the thought of Bobby carrying him to bed cause his cock to stir? *Strange.*

Nik moaned as he took the first bite of meatloaf. "Oh my god, this has become my new favourite place to eat." He licked his fork before he was aware Bobby was staring at him once again. "What? Do I have ketchup on my face?"

Bobby shook his head. "Nope. Guess I've just never heard someone enjoy meatloaf so much."

Nik rolled his eyes at himself. Could he possibly be any more socially awkward? "Sorry."

Bobby went back to his dinner, and Nik tried to keep his noises under control. He'd become so used to eating frozen dinners, he'd forgotten what real food tasted like. "What's the address of this place?"

"Why?"

"I want to find out if it's at all on my bus route," Nik admitted. He hadn't been kidding when he'd told Bobby it was his new favourite restaurant.

"Bus route? You don't have a car?" Bobby looked shocked.

"I'm a New Yorker. I don't even know how to drive, what would I do with a car? Besides, parking costs a fortune in the city."

Bobby finished his lunch and pushed his plate to the centre of the table. Nik missed his mouth with a forkful of food when the big man began to rub his own stomach.

Not only did the fork hurt like hell, but Bobby had witnessed the whole thing. *Yep. I'm socially awkward.* Deciding to quit while he was ahead, he signalled the waitress.

"All done?" the woman asked.

"Can I get a to-go box, please?" He'd managed to eat about a third of his lunch before embarrassing himself too badly. Better to take the rest home than risk further humiliation.

"You sure you've had enough?"

Nik nodded, thanking his lucky stars Bobby had stopped with the belly petting routine. "I'm fine. If I eat too much at a sitting I get an upset stomach."

"Well, we wouldn't want that. We've got a bott...er, cask to study."

Nik pulled his battered backpack closer and unzipped the side pocket to get to his wallet. He waited while Bobby studied the bill before reaching out to tally up his share.

"I got it." Bobby laid cash on the table along with the cheque.

"Don't be ridiculous. I can pay my half." He started to reach for the bill, but Bobby's hand landed on top of Nik's before he could grab the cheque.

"I got it," Bobby said again. "You can get the next one."

The wink Bobby bestowed shocked Nik to his core. Was he being flirted with? He released the slip of paper, but noticed Bobby appeared to be reluctant to remove his hand.

The waitress broke the moment by appearing with a take-out container. Bobby lifted his hand and slung his arm over the back of the booth, but he continued to maintain eye contact with Nik, until Nik finally looked away.

"Thanks." Nik took the container and filled it with his leftovers. By the time he had his meal safely tucked away, Bobby stood beside the table.

"Ready?"

Nik nodded and slid out of the booth. He felt the warmth of Bobby's hand against the small of his back as he made his way to the door. Nik wasn't even sure Bobby was aware he was doing it.

Once in the car, Nik tried to get his mind off the touch and back on the opportunity he had waiting for him at the police lab. "So they're going to let me remove the seal, right?"

"As long as you can assure me you know what you're doing, then yes."

There was something about the way Bobby said it that reminded him of his mother. Although he'd loved her until the day she died, Sorina Radin had never believed in him.

"Would it help if I ran down a list of my credentials? Because believe me, I've got them. You may think because I stick my cheek with a fork or moan when I eat really good food that I'm a simpleton, but I'm not! I've worked damn hard to get where I am today, and I won't let you or anyone else call my expertise into question."

Nik hadn't even realised Bobby had stopped the car until he was finished ranting. His head began to pound as he closed his eyes and rested it against the back of the seat.

"Look, I don't know what your issues are, but my ass is on the line. I'd question anyone before I gave them access to such a vital piece of evidence. Now just calm the fuck down."

Nik was too humiliated to say anything. An apology was on the tip of his tongue, but before he could say it, Bobby spoke once more.

"By the way, the moans and the fork in the cheek? Made me hard. I don't think you're a simpleton, I think you're probably a brilliant man who's spent too damn much time in the fucking library instead of out in the real world."

"You're right." Nik opened his eyes and gazed at Bobby. No way could he deny Bobby's observations, they were spot on. So much so it was actually kind of creepy. He'd yet to process the 'hard' comment, which he decided to file away for future exploration.

Bobby reached out and squeezed Nik's shoulder. "Are you ready to hold a five hundred and something year old cask?"

Nik nodded. He was grateful Bobby didn't seem to be the kind of guy to hold a grudge. If he were honest with himself he knew it was because he liked the guy that his words had hurt so much. Hopefully his foot-in-mouth disease wouldn't run Bobby off.

Chapter Five

Once inside the lab, Bobby showed Nik to a small room. "Wait here."

Nik nodded, taking a seat at the long conference table. Most of what he'd need was already there. He pulled a pair of nitrile gloves out of the provided box and adjusted the blacklight lamps before turning off the overhead fluorescent lights.

Bobby returned and held the door open for a technician. The tech set the cloth-covered cask carefully onto a wooden stand. Nik was pleased the guy took such care in transporting the fragile discovery.

"Do you mind if I stay?" The technician asked Nik.

"Not at all…"

"Peter Allenbrand," the tech provided.

Nik nodded and carefully removed the piece of cloth. A crest imbedded at the top of the wax caught his attention. "Oh, I didn't see this in the photograph."

"What?" Bobby leant over Nik's shoulder, getting a closer look at the seal.

"This crest. They were used in place of signatures." The more he examined the aging wax, the more worried he became. Nik glanced up at Bobby. "I don't think there's any way to get this off without breaking it."

"Shit." Bobby ran a hand over his short, dark blond hair. "What now?"

Nik turned to Peter. "Can you take some very detailed photographs of this for me?"

Peter looked to Bobby for permission. After Bobby nodded, the man wrapped the cask back up and carried it from the room.

Once they were alone, Bobby took a seat beside Nik. "So, what're your thoughts?"

"Well, the crest is definitely something I can research by using a photograph. I'd still like to know what's under the wax though." Nik thrummed his fingers against the table. He knew even if he got to the label it would most likely be stained to the point of being illegible. There had to be a way to get the cask to a restoration expert. It was a thing of beauty and deserved to be in a museum. A thought hit him. "I'm wondering if a call to the Mayor from an old professor of mine who now works at the Smithsonian would help."

"Help how? You've lost me."

"I know you can't go into details about the case you're working on, but this cask is one hell of a historic find. I'd be very interested to know how relevant it is to your case."

Bobby's hazel eyes narrowed to mere slits. "Why does that matter?"

"Because if I call my old professor, I've no doubt he could have the cask in his hands within twenty-four hours. I guess what I'm asking is will this cause you a problem with your investigation?"

Bobby sighed. "I probably shouldn't be telling you this, but frankly, I don't know how to answer your question. The cask was found in the study of Morgan Thompson on the night he was killed."

Nik swallowed. He'd read the details of the murderous rampage in the Times. He knew Thompson had murdered the servants in his household before venturing out onto the street, but that was about it. "Can I ask what made you think the cask was in any way connected?"

Bobby seemed uneasy. Nik knew it was difficult for the detective to discuss an open case.

"Please. It's important that I know, before I make my phone call."

"Evidence shows he'd been drinking from it on the night of the murders." Bobby's shoulders seemed to slump. "God, I'm so going to get fired for telling you that."

Nik shook his head. "It won't go any further, I promise."

"So do you have any ideas?"

"Well, I'm surprised as hell that anything was still in the cask in the first place. Since it appears there was, it surprises me further that someone actually drank it. It couldn't have been palatable."

Nik buried his face in his hands, something he often did when he was deep in thought. "It just doesn't make sense. A cask as unique as this one, still full of wine, or whatever, would be almost priceless, so why would someone intentionally devalue such an investment by drinking its contents?"

"That's why I figured it was a substantial clue. The lab is trying to analyse the contents."

"It's more than a clue, it's the reason. Don't ask me how I know, call it a gut instinct." Nik lifted his head and stared into the detectives eyes. "I think it's more important than ever to find out exactly where this cask came from and who made it, and the only way that's going to happen is to find out what's under that wax seal."

"So, what are you proposing?"

"That we get it to a restoration expert. I don't want to get you in hot water, so I figure an order from the Mayor to release the cask for expert analysis would help smooth things over with your boss."

"Let me give it some thought. It would go over better if I warned my lieutenant before she gets the actual phone call."

"Is there a way for you to speak to her now? I've no idea what'll be involved in finding out what's under that wax, but it'll most likely take some time. The quicker we get answers, the quicker you solve your case." Nik held his breath, waiting for Bobby's decision.

After several moments, Bobby stood and pulled his cell phone out of his jacket pocket. "I'll give it a shot. I sure hope you're right about this."

Nik reached out and grabbed Bobby's free hand, giving it a slight squeeze. "I wouldn't put you in this position if I wasn't sure."

Bobby pulled his hand away and left the room in mid-dial. Nik was surprised when the door opened a few seconds later. He turned to find Peter. "Oh. Did you get them?"

Peter held out several photographs. "That's the best I can do with what we have here. Is it enough?"

Nik studied the blown up images of the wax seal. "These are great. Thanks, Peter."

Peter left the room, and Nik continued to stare at the crest. *God, why did it look so familiar?* He reached for his backpack and withdrew a notebook and pencil. He was far from an artist, so he laid a blank sheet of paper over the photo and began to trace the image.

He was so involved in what he was doing, he didn't hear Bobby re-enter the room. The large hand landing on his shoulder caused him to jump.

"Shit. I'm sorry," Bobby apologised.

Nik shook his head and picked up his pencil from where it had dropped. "Did you talk to your boss?"

"Yeah. She's not happy, but she listened to everything I said, which is a good sign."

"So? What does that mean? Will she come down on you if I call Professor Lattimer?"

Bobby scratched at the back of his neck. "She said I'd better be right or it would be my head. That's as close to her blessing as I'm likely to get."

The drawing forgotten, Nik reached into his backpack for his phone. He searched his contact list and came up with George Lattimer's phone number. Now that Bobby had faced the dragon, it was Nik's turn.

"Hello?"

"Professor Lattimer? This is Nikolay Radin."

"Nikolay, how are you, boy?"

"I'm well, sir, and you?"

"Having the time of my life."

"That's good to hear, sir." He knew he needed to get to the point. George Lattimer was a talker, and Nik knew he could easily spend the next fifteen minutes discussing the weather. "The reason I'm calling is for your expertise."

"Really? I thought you were an expert now?" George chuckled.

"In some subjects, but I have a miniature cask from the mid-fifteenth century that I need help with."

"Is this for a class?"

"No, sir. I'm working with the NYPD." Nik went on to describe the cask. He didn't tell the professor any more than was absolutely necessary, but from the sounds of George's breathing on the other end of the phone, he didn't need to. Nik nodded his head at Bobby before he even finished his conversation. He knew his old professor was as excited by the find as Nik had been.

"...so I'd like to find out what's written on the label under the wax seal. Can you tell me how long you think that'll take you?"

"It would depend on how soon I can get it to DC and the severity of the staining."

"Do you think a call to the mayor would help speed the process?" Nik knew he was pushing, but George had never been known to back down from a challenge.

"Leave it to me. One way or another, I'll get it couriered down here as soon as possible. Now, about this crest, any idea who it belongs to?"

"Not yet. I have a feeling I'll be spending a few hours with my nose stuck in research books."

"Go to the New York Public Library on Forty-second Street and ask for Edna Grant. I'll give her a call and let her know you're coming."

"Thank you, Professor Lattimer."

"No, thank you, my boy. You may have dropped the find of the century into my lap."

Nik hung up and turned to Bobby. "He said to let him take care of it. I don't know who he'll call, but Professor Lattimer has some powerful connections in both Washington and New York."

Bobby nodded. "Okay, now what do we do?"

Nik held up the half-finished drawing. "I need to do some research. Would you mind dropping me by the library on Forty-second Street?"

"Not at all. Do you want some help?"

Nik knew his concentration would suffer with the gorgeous detective around, so he reluctantly shook his head. "I can do this part, but you'll be the first to know when I find something."

Bobby leant against the wall with his hands in his pockets while Nik gathered his things. It appeared as though the detective wanted to say something but was holding back. Nik assumed he was still worried about the cask, so he didn't push.

Nik held up the photographs. "Would it be okay if I take one of these?"

"Sure. I'll take the others and put them with the rest of the case files."

After zipping his backpack, he stood in front of Bobby. "I'm ready."

Bobby nodded and opened the door. Nik began to wonder if the detective was angry with him. He knew Bobby took a chance calling him in on the case in the first place. Maybe the detective regretted his decision.

He followed Bobby to the car and got in. The interior of the vehicle smelled of meatloaf and green beans. "Sorry," he apologised when Bobby climbed behind the wheel.

Chuckling, Bobby rolled down the window. "I'm not sure if that's going to be any good by the time you eat it."

Nik opened the container and looked at the leftovers. "I think it'll be fine."

Bobby steered the car in the direction of Forty-second Street. "So, how long will you be at the library?"

"It closes at six. Unfortunately, the books I'll be looking at are reference books and can't be checked out. They're closed on Sundays, so I'll have to try again Monday if I don't find what I need tonight."

The conversation ended and Bobby went back to looking uneasy. After several moments, Nik couldn't take it any longer. "I'm sorry I haven't been much help."

Bobby turned to look at Nik. "Why would you be sorry? You've got things in the works it would've taken me weeks to get going. And that's assuming I even knew what I was doing in the first place."

Nik shrugged. "I just got the feeling you were disappointed in me."

Bobby turned a corner. "No. I was just wondering if you'd like to go to the track with me tomorrow."

Is he asking me out on a date? "The horse track?"

"Yeah. I like to go at least once on the weekend when the horses are running. It's my way to relax."

"Oh, well, um, sure. I mean, I've never been, but it sounds fun." Nik knew he wouldn't actually bet on the horses. Gambling away money he'd worked hard to earn, never really made sense to him. But spending the day with the handsome detective sounded very appealing.

Bobby's mood seemed to lighten. "Good. How about if I pick you up around eleven?"

"That sounds good. It'll give me time to get my weekend chores finished." Of course it wouldn't leave time for grading. He thought of the large stack of papers on his kitchen table and gave an inward sigh. Maybe if he stayed up late he could get them done before class on Monday.

Bobby double parked in front of the library steps. "Sure you don't want me to stay and give you a ride home?"

Nik gathered his things. "Thanks, but I'm used to public transportation. It doesn't bother me."

"If it's dark, promise me you'll take a cab?"

Nik smiled at the detective's protective instincts. "Only if it's really dark."

Nik started to get out of the car, but Bobby reached out and grabbed his hand, holding him in place. "Seriously, Nik. Use the money you would've spent on lunch and take a cab."

Knowing he wouldn't win, Nik eventually nodded. "I promise."

Bobby released his hand and Nik climbed out onto the street. Taxis were honking as they tried to get around the detective's car. "You're going to get a ticket if you don't get moving."

Bobby winked. "I know people."

Nik shut the door and waved as Bobby drove away. He turned and made his way up the library steps. Trying to take his mind off the sexy detective and back to the task at hand, he thought of the crest.

Before going to the reference section, he sat at a table and tried to gather his thoughts. No sense going on a wild goose chase. There was something so familiar about the crest. He knew it was a matter of sorting through the information in his mind. He pulled the drawing and photograph out of his pack.

Outlining the picture with his finger, he let his mind wander. He knew the seal was two crests laid over the top of each other. He tried to visualise the separate images. Damn, if only the seal was clearer. It wasn't Peter's fault, he could barely make out the individual seals used to stamp across the hot wax, Nik believed it had been intentional. Whoever these seals belonged to didn't want their identity available to just anyone. *Why?*

He wondered if the archives held a book on family crests. Of course it could be the crest of a society or organisation. Nik gathered his things once again and went in search of Edna.

* * * *

By the time Nik arrived home he was starving. He quickly ate his leftovers from lunch as he pulled his notebook out of the backpack. Picking up the phone, he dialled Bobby's cell, excited to tell the detective what he'd found.

It rang several times before Bobby eventually answered. "Marks."

"Bobby, its Nik."

"Oh, I didn't recognise the number on the caller ID."

"I'm calling from home. Listen, I think I've got some good news. I can't be positive, but I think I found a reference to one of the crests."

"One of the crests?"

"Yeah. I figured out there are two crests, one pressed over the top of the other. That's why the image seems so distorted. Anyway, I'm not one hundred percent positive, but I believe one of the crests belongs to The Knights of Paiderastia."

"The Knights of what?"

"Paiderastia. It was a secret society that believed in religious fulfilment through the love of...boys." Nik felt his face flush.

"That's sick."

"Yeah, but the society was composed of some very powerful men at the time. One man in particular came to mind once I finally realised what I was seeing." Nik was practically vibrating in his excitement. If what he believed held true, the cask was even more valuable than he first thought.

"Okay, I'll bite, what man?"

The image of Bobby biting had Nik's cock filling in no time. He really did need to get out more. "Radu cel Frumos, better known as Radu Dracul. Radu happens to be the brother of the most famous resident of Romania outside of Nadia Comaneci, Vlad Dracul III."

Bobby didn't say anything, so Nik continued. "Vlad Dracul III is better known as…"

"Count Dracula," Bobby finished for him.

"Yes. That's what the books have made him into, but he was a real person."

Bobby went silent once again.

"Bobby? Is there something wrong?"

"I know it's getting late, but can I come over? There's something I need to talk to you about, and I'd rather not do it over the phone."

Nik's gaze went to the stack of papers he'd yet to grade. "Sure. I'll be here."

After hanging up with Bobby, Nik threw the remainder of his dinner in the trash, deciding Bobby had been right. He just hoped he didn't die of food poisoning before his big date tomorrow. *Oh. Shit.* Bobby was coming over.

Nik flew out of the kitchen and ran up the steps. He turned on the shower and started to shave while he waited for the water to heat. With his face smooth, he ducked under the hot spray. He quickly shampooed his hair and washed his other body parts thoroughly before drying off.

As he walked into his bedroom, water continued to drip off the black ringlets of his hair and down his chest and back. He opened his drawer and began to dress in his usual style of too-big sweat pants and an extra large T-shirt. There was something about baggy clothes that made him feel comfortable.

He stood at the foot of his bed and thought about making it just in case Bobby came up, but pushed the thought away. He'd never been the kind of guy to put out on a first date and they hadn't even gone on one of those yet.

As he made his way downstairs, he looked at the state of his living room and groaned. Cleaning was one of the chores he had planned for the day before Bobby had called him.

He gathered the dirty clothes from beside the sofa and ran them to the laundry room before starting on the newspapers. After those were tossed into the recycle bin came the dirty dishes that littered the coffee table.

"Well, there *is* an actual table under there," he commented with a giggle. As long as he kept Bobby in the living room, hopefully the detective wouldn't think he was too much of a slob.

By the time the doorbell rang, Nik was worn out. He brushed his wayward curls out of his face and opened the door. "Hi."

"Hey," Bobby greeted with a grin.

Nik stepped back. "Come in."

He led Bobby into the living room. "Can I get you something to drink?"

"Sure, whatever you're having is fine."

Nik gestured to the couch. "Make yourself comfortable. I'll be right back."

He rushed to the kitchen and opened the fridge. He hoped he had a bottle of wine left over from the previous holiday season. Squatting down, he searched the shelves. *Damn.*

His choices were cherry Kool-Aid or apple juice. He wondered if he had coffee. That was a more grown up drink, right? He was standing in front of the refrigerator chewing on his thumbnail when he heard Bobby step into the room.

"Everything okay?"

Nik pointed at the fridge. "I was trying to figure out what to get you."

Bobby stepped up behind him and put his hands on Nik's shoulders. "Juice would be fine."

Instead of pulling the juice out of the open refrigerator, Nik stayed where he was, relishing in the warmth of Bobby's touch. He turned his head and tilted it up. *Oh God, oh god, oh god.*

Bobby lowered his head and pressed his lips against Nik's. The kiss was gentle, but sure, just like Bobby. Nik turned and threaded his fingers through the back of Bobby's hair as he opened his mouth.

A moan escaped him as Bobby's tongue swept the interior of his mouth. The sound seemed to fuel the kiss even more as Bobby wrapped his arms around Nik's waist and pulled him in.

Snug against the big detective's body, Nik couldn't imagine a better place to be. He brushed his tongue against Bobby's, getting in on the erotic play.

Bobby was the first to pull back, breaking the kiss. He stared down into Nik's eyes and smiled. "I actually didn't come here for this, but I couldn't help myself."

"I'm glad you find me irresistible," Nik teased.

"I do. There's just something about you that fascinates me."

"Well feel free to study me anytime you'd like."

Bobby loosened his hold on Nik. "We really do need to talk."

"Okay," Nik whispered before standing on his toes for another brief kiss. Although Bobby kissed him back, Nik could feel a bit of tension creeping into the man's shoulders. He broke the kiss and stepped away from the temptation. "Two glasses of juice, coming up."

He grabbed the bottle out of the fridge and carried it to the counter. After filling two glasses, he led Bobby back into the living room. His lips felt swollen from their momentary lapse in restraint and Nik couldn't have been happier about it.

Nik was even more pleased when Bobby sat towards the centre of the sofa and patted the space beside him.

"Tell me again about this Radu guy."

His research. *Yes. Okay.* "Um, well, Radu was the half-brother of Vlad III or Vlad the Impaler as he became known."

Bobby took a drink and nodded. "Sorry, I'm just trying to get my head back to the reason I came."

"Take your time." Nik couldn't resist licking his lips, hoping to taste Bobby's kiss.

"That's not helping," Bobby practically growled.

"Oops. Sorry." Nik sat up straight and put his hands in his lap. "Go on."

"There's something I think you should know. We've somehow managed to keep a few of the more gory details out of the news, but I think it's relevant to your research."

Nik leaned closer, like a boy waiting to hear a secret. "Okay."

"After Morgan Thompson killed his victims, he drank their blood."

Nik gasped. There were quickly becoming too many references to the Dracul family in this investigation. He hated to sound like a know-it-all, but he just had to say it. "I told you the cask was the key to solving this case."

Bobby nodded.

"Now that I know a few of your secrets, will you share another with me?" Nik asked.

"If I can," Bobby answered easily.

"Where'd the cask come from?"

"It appears that Thompson bought it at an auction. My partner, Jablonsky, has been checking out the auction houses, but so far he's come up empty."

Nik shook his head. "This cask wasn't purchased at your normal auction. If a place like Christies had something as valuable as this on the block, you'd better believe it would've been all over the news. Tell your partner to look into black market auctions or private collector sales. If you're lucky, maybe you can track down the seller. Why release a five hundred and fifty year-old cask of wine now? There has to be a reason."

"What does the wine have to do with the Draculs?"

"I don't know. How long before the lab has the content analysis done?"

"I'm not sure. I can check on it Monday. Wilmont will kill me if I call and interrupt his Sunday with the family. To be honest, I haven't really been pushing that hard. I mean, I thought it was wine. I was trying to determine if it was poisoned or something."

"My guess is 'or something'."

Chapter Six

Water dripped from Bobby's chest as he stood in front of his closet, wrapped in a towel, and trying to decide what to wear. He heaved a frustrated breath before grabbing the first shirt and pair of jeans his hands touched. Somewhere between the previous night and the time he stepped from his shower, he started channelling a sixteen-year-old girl. It was the most logical explanation for why he couldn't find one fucking outfit that he liked.

"Outfits," he muttered, tossing his clothes on the bed before digging in his drawers for socks and underwear.

That thought solidified his belief in his channelling a girl because he didn't have outfits; he had jeans or suits. He wasn't the kind of guy who put a lot of thought into his wardrobe. Suits were a must for work, ever since the Commissioner instituted a dress code for detectives. Bobby bought good quality suits, but they weren't Armani, that was for sure.

He tugged on his boxer-briefs and sat on the bed to put on his socks. He caught sight of the sweats he'd worn earlier while he worked out. Those ragged things brought Nik to the forefront of his mind.

God, the professor was pretty, but obviously didn't know it, dressing in baggy sweats and over-sized T-shirts. Nik had a lean little body, which Bobby discovered when he'd kissed the man the previous night. They shouldn't have kissed, Bobby knew that, but he couldn't resist. Nik had smelled so clean and fresh and Bobby had wanted to taste Nik's lips since the moment they'd met.

The memory of how Nik threw himself into their kiss stiffened Bobby's cock and he carefully zipped his jeans up, not wanting to cause bodily harm. A quick glance at the clock next to his bed brought a soft curse from him.

He was going to be late if he didn't speed things up a little. Bobby slipped his T-shirt on and raced out into the living room, searching for his boots. Ah, there they were. He snatched them up and stuffed his feet into them. Sunglasses on his face, keys in hand, phone clipped to his belt, and wallet in his back pocket. He chose to leave his off-duty gun behind. His gut told him Nik might be unnerved if he found out Bobby carried a weapon even when he wasn't working.

Bobby shrugged as he slammed his apartment door shut. If something bad happened, it wasn't like he couldn't handle the situation. Running down the stairs, he waved to his neighbours as he passed them. Out the back of the building to where he parked his beloved car.

He paused in his head-long flight to appreciate the clean lines of the Camaro. 1969, the year the stars aligned and Chevrolet built the perfect muscle car. Bobby had lovingly restored the entire car and now it was his prized possession. He ran his hand over the roof of the car as he opened the door.

"No one will ever take your place in my heart, darling," he cooed as he slipped behind the wheel and let the leather seats welcome him.

The engine roared to life and he grinned. What red-blooded, All-American male wouldn't grin at the sound of that? He pressed the heel of his hand against his erection threatening to break through his jeans. Oh yeah, and what guy didn't get hard at the thought of all that power?

He buckled up, turned the radio on, and backed out of his parking spot. The metal gate clanked open after he punched in his code. One of the reasons he chose this particular apartment building was because of the fenced-in lot. There wasn't any way he'd leave his baby out on the street where it could get scratched or dented.

Merging into traffic, he headed towards Chelsea, praying traffic was light. He'd hate to be late on their first date. A good first impression lent itself to the possibility of more dates, and Bobby wanted to get to know Nik better.

His phone rang and he grabbed it from the console where he'd thrown it when he got in the car.

"Marks."

"Hey partner," Jablonsky's gruff voice roared over the phone.

"Shit. I forgot to call you. I got some good information on that cask we found at the Thompson place."

"Already?" His partner laughed. "We'll be the lieutenant's favourite detectives."

He doubted it, but didn't comment on that. "Yeah, get this. It's over five hundred years old and might have belonged to Dracula's half-brother."

"Dracula? Like 'I'm going to suck your blood' Dracula?"

"Crazy shit, huh?" Stopping at a light, he tapped his fingers on the steering wheel. "It might explain Thompson drinking his victims' blood after he killed them."

"Yeah right. Did you try that theory on the lieutenant? I bet she didn't buy it either. More than likely, whatever wine was in that bottle was poisoned and it fried his brain."

"Cask," he muttered, accelerating through traffic.

"All those vampire stories were made-up, man, to make Dracula, or whatever his real name was, seem scary to his enemies." Jablonsky grunted. "Do you have any useful information?"

"Oh, my expert says you should look at black market auctions or private sales because the cask alone is priceless, so if Christies or Sotheby's sold something like that, the public would know about it." He shifted in his seat. "We'll probably be called on the carpet tomorrow."

Jablonsky sighed. "What for?"

Even though Bobby tried to stay under the lieutenant's radar, he and Jablonsky got more than their fair share of verbal ass-kicking.

"Our lieutenant will be receiving a phone call from somebody important, I'm sure, and ordered to release our cask into the hands of a restoration expert at the Smithsonian."

"You didn't okay it with her first?"

Bobby nodded, forgetting Jablonsky couldn't see him. "Yeah, I did sort of. I asked her about removing the seal and sending it to another expert. She wasn't thrilled about it."

"I bet." A soft sigh crept over the phone. "If your gut's telling you that letting some expert look at it is the right track for our case, I'll back you and, you know that the lieutenant will take the heat for us as long as it brings us results. Now, I'm hanging up and getting ready for brunch with the family. You have fun at the track."

"See you tomorrow, Jablonsky."

He flipped the phone shut and tossed it in the passenger seat. Traffic was surprisingly light for the city, so he pulled up in front of Nik's house right on time. Climbing out, he stretched for a moment and looked around. The houses were older, probably built by the men who worked the docks or in the meat packing plant. Being a professor must earn Nik some serious cash because realty prices in Chelsea were high, now that the section of town was desirable again.

Bobby jogged up the front steps and knocked on the door. He leaned against the doorframe, watching people wander down the sidewalk.

"Hey, Bobby."

Turning, he smiled and shoved his sunglasses to the top of his head. "Nik."

Without really considering his actions, he leant forward and brushed a kiss over Nik's lips. Those gorgeous dark green eyes Nik kept hidden behind his glasses widened in surprise. Bobby pulled back before he was tempted to take the kiss further.

"You feel lucky today?"

Nik hesitated before nodding and joining Bobby out on the porch. Even though he watched Nik lock the door, he couldn't help reaching around him and testing to make sure it latched. Nik eyed him as they headed towards his car.

"Sorry. Occupational hazard, I guess." He shrugged and opened the passenger side door for Nik.

"It's okay. I just don't want you to think I'm so scatterbrained that I wouldn't remember to lock my own house." Nik frowned.

Bobby shut the door and ran around the car to get in. Before he started the car, he turned to look at Nik. He reached out and cradled the man's face in his hands.

"I think you're the kind of guy who gets caught up in a book or an interesting piece of research and forgets to eat. You might forget where you left your backpack or cell phone, but I don't think that makes you scatterbrained. I think that makes you intensely focused and I find that a total turn-on."

Resisting temptation had never been one of Bobby's strong suits. Lifting Nik's chin a little more, he brought his lips close to Nik's and ran his tongue over the seam of Nik's mouth, asking for permission. Nik moaned slightly and opened for Bobby. Eager for another taste, Bobby plunged his tongue in, learning all the nooks and crannies of Nik's mouth, teasing Nik's tongue into his own mouth, and sucking on it.

Nik trembled, and his hands lay, clenched in his lap. Bobby eased back a few inches and whispered, "You can touch me if you want."

His words seemed to break Nik's control and the man launched himself into Bobby's arms, wiggling like he wanted to climb onto Bobby's lap. The steering wheel stopped that from happening, but Bobby made a silent vow not to let too much time go by before he experienced Nik straddling his thighs.

The kiss heated up and became sloppy as they teased each other with teeth, tongues, and lips. Bobby threaded his fingers into Nik's hair, holding the younger man still while he plundered his mouth.

Only when his lungs screamed for oxygen did he back off. Nik's face was flushed and his eyes hazy with lust. The front of Nik's khakis didn't hide the bulge of the man's erection. Smiling, Bobby helped Nik back into his seat and fastened the seat belt while Nik caught his breath and seemed to get his body under control.

"Shit. I knew you were going to be a firecracker." Bobby inhaled deeply, enjoying the scent of desire and need filling his car. "If I hadn't needed to breathe, our first time would have been in the backseat of my car, and trust me, that isn't comfortable."

Nik ducked his head, cheeks beet red. Bobby reached out and caressed Nik's cheekbone.

"I think our first time should be in a bed with all the time in the world. I want to lick every inch of you and have you screaming my name by the time I'm done with you."

His crude words seemed to have shocked Nik, because the professor didn't comment as Bobby started the car and pulled away from the kerb. He turned the radio up, letting classic rock pour out of the speakers. He took Nik's hand and rested it on his thigh under his own.

"Which track are we going to?" Nik's voice was hoarse.

"Belmont. It's their fall meet. I only go up to Saratoga when I have a couple days in a row off, and I know I'm not going to get called in." Bobby squeezed Nik's hand. "Got some good horses running today. I'll teach you how to pick a winner."

"I don't gamble."

"You won't even wager a dollar?" He drove with easy confidence, knowing just how tightly tuned his car was.

"I work hard for my money. Why would I want to throw it away on a horse race?" Nik frowned.

Bobby winked at Nik. "See, I knew you were smarter than me. I don't bet a lot of money. Don't wanna have to sell my car to pay my debts. It took me too long to restore this beauty to lose it all on a bet."

Twenty minutes later, they were parking at Belmont and Bobby led Nik in through the gates. After grabbing a programme and the Daily Racing Form, he rested his hand at the small of Nik's back and directed the smaller man through the crowd to the grandstands.

Track regulars called out to him, asking him who he picked to win the first race. He joked with them, but didn't stop. Nik's shoulders were tense and Bobby got the feeling that Nik didn't get out much and crowds might make the professor nervous.

"Don't worry. This is my favourite spot, right at the finish. We'll get a good look at the horses crossing the line." He gestured for Nik to take a seat. "Are you hungry or thirsty? I can get us something."

Nik shook his head, his gaze wandering over the crowd. What was Nik thinking? Did he regret coming to the track with Bobby? Was the noise and the people overwhelming for the man?

Bobby sat down and gripped Nik's shoulder. "If you get bored or decide you've had enough, let me know. I come here every weekend, so leaving early wouldn't be a problem for me."

Nik nodded and Bobby decided to relax. Nik was a big boy and he'd tell Bobby if he wasn't happy. Opening the programme, he checked which horses were running in the first race. He handed it to Nik and folded the Form open, flipping through the pages until he got to the Beyer Speed Figures.

"Okay, Nik. Are you ready for your first lesson in betting on the horses?"

Biting his lip, Nik wrinkled his nose and Bobby laughed.

"Don't worry. I'm not going to frog-march you up to the windows and force you to place a bet. I'll do the betting." He bumped their shoulders together. "Who knows? Maybe you'll be good luck for me."

Nik didn't look convinced, but it didn't bother Bobby. It was a gorgeous fall day and he had a hot man at his side. He pushed all thoughts of the case out of his head for the time being. Tomorrow would be soon enough for him to get back to working on the Thompson murders.

* * * *

Nik grinned as Bobby handed him his winnings. "Beginner's luck."

Bobby slapped the rolled programme in his hand against his thigh and took his seat. "Yeah, well three straight wins is pushing the beginner's luck thing a little far."

Feeling comfortable for the first time since they arrived at the track, Nik leaned against Bobby's side. "Well, you don't have to worry about me anymore. I'm done. I'll take my mountains of cash and buy us a hamburger after we leave."

Bobby swung his arm to the back of Nik's seat and cupped his shoulder. "I still say picking a horse by the colour isn't a smart way to bet."

Nik inched even closer to Bobby's warmth. If they'd been alone, he definitely would've tried everything in his arsenal to get Bobby's mind off the races. He could tell Bobby knew what he was doing when it came to placing bets, but the detective's luck seemed to have been left in the car.

With his free hand, Bobby opened the programme and began studying the race after the one getting ready to be run. It was nice being with someone who wasn't afraid to show a little affection in public.

Nik had never gone for making out or anything like that around the straights, but holding hands or simply wrapping his arms around a lover seemed natural. Why should he hide his feelings just because they made some people uncomfortable?

Evidently, Bobby wasn't the only one losing, because the stands slowly emptied as the races continued. It suited Nik just fine. He knew it was strange for a man born and raised in a city to feel overwhelmed by large crowds, but he'd grown up in his small corner of Chelsea. His parents had barely managed to pay the bills on the home he still lived in. Traipsing around Manhattan hadn't been a luxury they could afford, so Nik spent the majority of his time either in his room or the local branch of the library.

Bobby hugged Nik closer to his side. "You doing okay?"

Nik gave in to temptation and rested his hand on Bobby's flat stomach. "Does it bother you if I sit this close?"

Bobby chuckled, and leant down to whisper in Nik's ear. "The only thing it's bothering is my dick."

Nik licked his lips. "I can't do much about that here, sorry."

For a brief moment, Bobby nuzzled Nik's ear. "As soon as this next race has been run, why don't we get out of here?"

Nik nodded. What was it about the detective that made him feel different from any other man he'd been with?

Normally, he was reserved when it came to jumping into the sack. It was only about three hours into his first official date with Bobby, and he was more than ready to jump the man's bones. He was so lost in his fantasies, he didn't even realise the horses were ready until it was over.

Bobby growled and tossed his ticket to the ground, before standing. "My luck is complete shit today."

Nik stood and grabbed Bobby's hand as they walked towards the parking lot. Once they were far enough from the crowd, Nik stopped and pulled Bobby's head down for a quick kiss. "I've a feeling your luck is about to change."

Without a word, Bobby once again started towards his car, only this time it was more like running. Nik held tight to Bobby's hand and tried to keep up. In a sea of cars, Bobby managed to find the Camaro.

The moment they reached the car, Bobby pressed Nik against the passenger door and ravaged his mouth, sweeping the interior with that delicious tongue Nik was beginning to crave. Nik let out a soft whimper and Bobby pressed his thigh between Nik's legs, giving him something to grind against.

Holy fuck. Nik didn't know if he'd be able to make it somewhere secluded before shooting in his pants. "Need you."

Bobby reached between them and covered Nik's cock with his hand. "Can you maintain this for the twenty-five minutes it takes to get to my place?"

Nik laughed and kissed Bobby again. "I've had it the entire time we've been here, what's another twenty-five minutes."

Bobby groaned and pulled away. "Get in."

Nik followed orders and reached across the console to unlock Bobby's door, before fastening his seatbelt. He practically vibrated with lust, but he knew New York City traffic didn't lend itself to groping, so he sat on his hands to keep from reaching for the bulge pressing against Bobby's fly.

Leaving the track, Nik realised he didn't even know where Bobby lived. "So, where are we headed?"

"Bronx." Bobby didn't even look over at Nik as he said it.

If it weren't for the prominent erection, he might think Bobby was mad. The white-knuckled grip Bobby had on the steering wheel told Nik the detective was also trying to keep himself in check. The thought of pushing Bobby's control excited Nik.

As soon as Bobby got on Cross Island Parkway, Nik released one of his hands from under his ass and ran it over his cock. At first he didn't think Bobby noticed, so he did it again, applying more pressure and giving himself the slightest squeeze.

"Stop it," Bobby growled.

Nik giggled. He couldn't remember ever having so much fun on a first date. With his seatbelt still in place, Nik turned his body towards Bobby. He gave his cock a purposeful grope and moaned. "Does this bother you?"

"Let's put it this way, you're about thirteen minutes from getting that tempting ass of yours spanked."

Nik's jaw dropped. Would Bobby really do it? Nik hadn't received a spanking since he was a boy. His shock must have shown on his face because Bobby started to chuckle.

The bigger man reached over and ran a hand up Nik's thigh, stopping just short of his groin. "Does it turn you on to think of my hand coming down on your bare ass?"

Nik swallowed around the lump in his throat. "I don't know. I mean, I don't think so."

Bobby took his eyes off the road long enough to glance at Nik. "What? You've never had a lover spank you?"

Nik felt his face flush. "No. Not that there've been many lovers, but maybe I didn't piss them off enough to spank me."

Bobby laughed harder. "It has nothing to do with pissing me off."

"Then why would you hit me?" Naïve he may be, but Nik didn't understand the draw of allowing a lover to hurt him.

Bobby turned off the parkway and merged into the Saturday traffic, before turning onto a side street. "Okay, no spankings. Remind me to talk to you about those later. The main thing you need to know is never to let someone do it to you in anger. It can be intense, but it has to be enjoyable for both partners or it won't work."

Nik subtly turned back to face front. He didn't even find the idea appealing. He couldn't imagine doing it for pleasure. Sounded kind of sick to him, but he decided to withhold judgement until a later date.

The conversation had somehow managed to alleviate some of the pressure in his underwear. Nik wasn't worried. He knew the second Bobby touched him, he'd be back to hard and needy.

He studied the neighbourhoods as they drove through. It wasn't often that he'd been to this side of the city. "This is nice," he commented.

Bobby pulled up to a big security gate and rolled his window down. He tapped a few numbers into the keypad and the gate opened. He pulled into what looked to be a reserved spot and shut off the engine.

Before opening the door, Bobby reached out and pulled Nik forward by the back of the neck. Bobby's mouth slammed down on his, thrusting his tongue inside. He finished the kiss with a soft bite to Nik's bottom lip. "Let's go."

Nik opened his door and climbed out, making sure to lock it. He checked the handle just to make sure before rounding the back of the car and wrapping his arm around Bobby's waist.

After using his key, they entered a small lobby, complete with mailboxes. Bobby pointed towards the stairs. "Third floor."

They started up the stairs with Nik leading the way. "There's no elevator?"

"Yeah, but it only works every second Tuesday. Better to take the stairs than chance getting trapped for hours."

By the time they got to the second floor, Bobby's hands kept reaching out to pat and pinch Nik's ass. Once they were outside Bobby's apartment, Nik was hard as a rock.

They barely made it inside, before Bobby locked the door and pulled his T-shirt over his head. "Strip."

The first thing Nik did was to remove his glasses and carefully set them on the entertainment centre. He turned back to Bobby and almost swallowed his tongue. Clad only in boxer-briefs, Bobby was stretched out on the couch, staring at him.

Nik's fingers began fumbling with the buttons of his blue cotton shirt. "Sorry. I learned a very important lesson growing up about my glasses. I tend to be a bit anal when it comes to taking care of them."

As he talked, Nik managed to remove his shirt. He toed off his old loafers and started on the zipper of his khakis. He pushed his pants down, eyes riveted to Bobby's hand as it rubbed and pulled on the long, thick cock trapped underneath his briefs.

Nik started to lunge for Bobby's package and tripped over the pants still trapped around his ankles. As he began to fall, Nik tried desperately to right himself before he went face-first into the coffee table.

A strong pair of arms scooped him up a split second before impact. Nik gazed into Bobby's eyes and grinned. "Oops."

Bobby tossed Nik onto the couch like he weighed nothing. Bobby came down over top of Nik and shook his head. "A trip to the emergency room isn't exactly what I had in mind."

"Lucky you caught me then." Nik wrapped his legs around Bobby's torso, bringing their cloth covered erections into contact.

With their cocks grinding against one another and Bobby's added height, Nik began kissing and licking his soon-to-be lover's neck.

Bobby groaned as Nik playfully bit the soft skin under his ear. "No bruises, at least not there."

"Mmmm." Nik released the skin and gave Bobby's body a slight push. "Let me on top, so I get at a spot I *can* mark."

Bobby sat back on his heels, and waited for Nik to move out from under him. Nik couldn't help but to grope the front of Bobby's tented underwear as they repositioned themselves.

With Bobby flat on the couch, Nik climbed aboard, straddling the bigger man's hips. He rested his ass against the hard ridge of Bobby's cock and began to slowly move as he traced Bobby's nipples with his fingertips.

"So…" Nik scraped his short fingernail across the pebbled nub. "Would this be an acceptable place for a bruise?"

Bobby gave him a lopsided grin. "For now."

Nik bent down and ran the flat of his tongue over the light brown nipple, before taking the nub between his teeth. He didn't bite down hard, just enough to elicit a moan from Bobby. He grinned to himself as he latched on to the sensitive skin.

Bobby pushed Nik's underwear down enough to run a finger along his crease. Nik released the nipple in his mouth and stared down at the darkening red spot. *Perfect.* "Is there another acceptable location?"

"You're sitting on it," Bobby answered, pressing the pad of his finger against Nik's hole.

"Hmmm, how do you feel about numbers?" Nik asked.

"Numbers?"

"Yes. The number sixty-nine to be exact."

Bobby smacked Nik's ass. "That's my favourite number."

Crawling off Bobby's lap, Nik stood and pushed down his underwear. He gestured to Bobby's briefs. "May I?"

Bobby nodded. His gaze zeroed in on Nik's stiff dick and licked his lips. "Depends on how fast you can do it, because I'm feeling awfully hungry."

Nik walked to the end of the couch and reached up to pull Bobby's briefs down. As soon as he had them off, Bobby trapped Nik's cock between his bare feet. Nik glanced down at the perfect feet jacking him off. "Kinky."

Bobby chuckled and flicked Nik's sac with his big toe. "Just playing with that beautiful cock of yours."

Valuing his jewels, Nik pulled back and shook his finger. He walked around to the opposite end of the couch and crawled down Bobby's body until his mouth was able to engulf the ruddy, mushroom-shaped head.

The taste of Bobby's pre-cum exploded on Nik's tongue. *God, kill me now.* He groaned as Bobby's cell phone rang. "Do you have to answer it?"

Bobby released Nik's testicle. "Unfortunately, it comes with the job."

Since he was on top, Nik scrambled off the couch and grabbed Bobby's jeans. "Here, catch."

After performing his duty, Nik went back to Bobby's cock, placing small licks along the heavily veined shaft. "This thing is truly a work of art."

Chuckling, Bobby put his finger over his lips as he answered the phone. "Marks."

Nik began to roll the lightly furred balls in his hand, half-listening to Bobby's conversation.

"What?" Bobby sat straight up on the couch, dislodging Nik.

"When?"

Nik could tell by Bobby's expression that something bad had happened. He knelt on the floor beside Bobby, resting his head against his lover's side.

"I'll be right there." Bobby's voice was low and troubled. He hung up the phone and rested a hand on Nik's head, idly plucking at Nik's curls. "They found a woman in a high-rise downtown. She's been drained of blood by a cut to her throat."

Chapter Seven

Bobby stood, taking care not to knock Nik over. Leaning down, he held out a hand to his soon-to-be lover.

"I have to jump in the shower. Can you pick out a suit for me?"

Nik seemed surprised that Bobby would ask him that, but Bobby dragged him back to his bedroom and pointed to the closet.

"Whatever you think looks good is fine. I'm going to a murder scene, not the opera."

He waited to see Nik nod before rushing into the bathroom. Shivering as he shut off the cold water, he determined he didn't have enough time to shave. *Screw it.* It was his day off, so the lieutenant would just have to deal with it. Bobby and Jablonsky weren't supposed to catch a case this weekend, but since it looked like the Thompson murders, the responding officers must have decided they needed to be there.

His teeth got a quick brush and he dried his short hair with a brisk rub of the towel. Heading back into his bedroom, he spotted Nik sitting on the bed, dressed.

Disappointment surged through Bobby. Damn. He was just going to get a piece of that sweet little ass and some psycho had to screw everything up.

Tugging out a clean pair of underwear and socks, he grinned at Nik. "The joys of dating a detective. Never know when you'll be interrupted."

"It's all right." Nik picked at his thumb, a habit Bobby had noticed the first day they met. "I just hope it doesn't have anything to do with your case."

Bobby reached out and covered Nik's hand, stopping him from doing more damage to the wound. "So do I, because if it's the same, that means it didn't have anything to do with the wine, or there are more casks out there that we don't know about."

Nik looked about as happy as Bobby felt at that thought. After dressing, Bobby removed his gun from the nightstand and clipped it on his belt. His badge went on the other side and he twitched his jacket down over them.

He gestured for Nik to follow him as he wandered back into the living room, looking for his dress shoes. Where had he kicked them off yesterday? Ah, there they were. Picking them up, he turned and saw Nik slip his shoes on.

"Where are you going?"

"I thought I'd head home. No point in sticking around since I have no idea when you'll be home." Nik's polite side must have been rearing its head.

Bobby sat, put his shoes on, and tied the laces while he studied Nik. Finally, he suggested, "Why don't you just stay here? I have food in the refrigerator and stuff to drink. You can watch movies, though all of mine are mostly black and whites from the thirties and forties."

"Why would you want me to stay?" Nik slid his glasses off and started polishing them on the hem of his shirt.

Was that another nervous trait? Bobby wasn't sure how he felt about making Nik nervous. He strolled up to the slender man, set his glasses back on his nose, and embraced him.

Nuzzling into the crook of Nik's neck, he breathed deep of the fresh outdoorsy scent Nik's skin held. Spending some of the day outside at the track—wandering the paddock area to look at the horses—lent Nik an intriguing smell mingled pleasantly with the scent of sweat and sex.

He licked a line up to the sensitive spot behind Nik's ear and sucked, just a little, and he swallowed a chuckle as Nik moaned and went limp, his trust in Bobby's strength implicit in his actions. His head tilted to give Bobby more access, Nik held tight to Bobby's shoulders. One more suck, a nibble to Nik's earlobe, and Bobby set the other man away from him.

"I want you to stay, so we can pick up where we were so rudely interrupted when I get back." He winked and leered at Nik.

A pretty blush coloured Nik's cheeks and Bobby couldn't resist swooping in for another fast, hard kiss.

"Will you stay?"

Nik glanced around the living room like he was searching for the answer to the question of life. Bobby cupped his face and smiled.

"If you don't feel comfortable here, I'll take you home. I'm not letting you ride the bus. That's not how my dad taught me to take care of my dates."

Inhaling deeply, Nik straightened his shoulders and nodded. "I'll stay."

"Good."

Bobby hugged him tight for a second before heading towards the door. "The remotes are on the end table closest to the TV. They're really easy to figure out. You're welcome to watch any of my movies you want."

He grabbed his keys, phone, and wallet as he raced by the hallway table on his way out the door. Pausing, he turned around and said, "Keep the door locked. I'll have my phone so call me if you need anything."

Nik nodded, looking slightly bewildered, but Bobby didn't have any more time to explain things to him. He slammed the door shut, checked to make sure it was locked, and ran down the back stairs to the door leading into the parking lot.

Shit, Jablonsky was going to kill him for not getting there sooner. Bobby shrugged as he pulled out of the lot and headed downtown. He dialled his partner's cell phone.

"Jablonsky."

"Hey, I'm on my way. Where am I going?"

"505 Central Park West. Apartment 8B." Jablonsky didn't sound happy.

Bobby whistled softly. "High society. Has the victim been identified yet?"

"Yeah, and you won't believe this."

Jablonsky muttered something to someone before getting back to Bobby.

"Who is it?" Bobby drummed his fingers on the steering wheel, wishing he had installed some sirens or lights in his car. Traffic wasn't stalled, but it wasn't moving at a fast clip either.

"Mavis Vanderlist."

"Holy shit!" Bobby closed his eyes for a brief second as all the ramifications of this murder flooded his head. Even Bobby had heard of Mavis, and the elite crowd she ran with.

"Yeah, partner. Only daughter of Reinholt Vanderlist. Old New York money and one of society's most popular celebrities."

"We are so screwed on this one, especially if it follows the same M.O. as the Thompson murders."

He pulled up to the apartment building with a barricade of marked police cars in front of it.

"I'm here. I'll be up in a minute."

After flipping his phone shut, he tucked it in his pocket and rested his forehead on the back of his hands, which were wrapped around the steering wheel. He took a few deep breaths. The media was going to be all over this and he had a feeling City Hall was going to start poking around as well. When someone like Mavis Vanderlist — who had rock star status in New York — was murdered, other people tended to take notice.

Do your job, Robert. That's all you can do, and let the chips fall where they may when the time comes. His father's voice echoed through his head, and Bobby nodded.

He slid from his car and held up his badge as he approached the two uniform cops guarding the entrance to the apartment building.

"Another fucking mess, Marks," Hansen said as Bobby walked past him.

"How'd you get so lucky as to draw both cases, Hansen?"

The older man shrugged. "Someone up there must really love me."

"Yeah, right. More like you pissed someone off, and now they're getting back at you."

Hansen's chuckle followed him as he strolled through the lobby to the elevator. Unlike the one at his apartment,

Bobby had no doubt this elevator was in prime working order.

When he stepped onto the eighth floor, he glanced down the hallway to where a crowd of cops and crime scene techs stood just outside the door of Apartment 8B. Jablonsky peered around the bodies and crooked his finger at Bobby.

"Marks, get your ass in here. I didn't let the techies touch anything until you arrived."

He pulled out a pair of nitrate gloves he kept in all his suit pockets and slid them on before taking a pair of booties from one of the lab guys. With no one getting inside, except the first responding uniforms, they couldn't take the chance of contaminating the evidence, if there was any left.

Stepping into the apartment, the first smell that hit Bobby's nose was the almost overwhelming metallic scent of blood. He glanced down and pointed at a trail of bloody footprints leading down the hallway from a back room.

"Rookie uniform. Stepped in the blood before he realised what it was. The head techie already chewed him out for not taking his shoes off immediately. I guess we should be lucky the guy held his lunch long enough to get out of the apartment." Jablonsky jerked a thumb over his shoulder towards the corridor where the others waited. "The cleaning staff aren't going to be happy about that."

Bobby grunted, but didn't comment. It wasn't like he hadn't vomited on his first violent and bloody murder. After a while, he got used to it, and so would the rookie, if he lasted on the force.

"Body's in the back bedroom."

Leading the way, he didn't look around. He wanted to see the body and the room first, then let the CSI guys in there. He and Jablonsky halted in the doorway and Bobby exhaled softly.

"We're not just screwed, partner. We're completely fucked."

He couldn't disagree. Mavis Vanderlist lay crumpled on the floor next to the bed, her eyes staring up blankly at the ceiling. The CSI guys would have to determine what colour her dress was before she died, because now it was dark red, saturated with her life's blood. She lay in a large dark pool of the stuff and it looked like she had to have bled out quickly.

"There's no way to approach her without stepping in the blood," he observed, needing to check the wound in her neck, but not wanting to disturb the scene.

"So we look around the rest of the apartment while the CSI rats take care of the evidence in here." Jablonsky backed out and turned, gesturing for the techies to come in. "Get everything bagged and tagged asap. We'll need detailed photographs as well."

"Yes, sir." Libby saluted as she snuck past, camera in hand.

Jablonsky rolled his eyes, but let her go by before heading towards the living room. Bobby stayed put, waving his hand to get Libby's attention.

"I want a close up of the wound to the neck."

Her gaze sharpened. "You think this might be related to the Thompson murders?"

"I can't say anything at the moment, but the similarities are striking." He spun around on his heel and followed Jablonsky.

"What is it about rich people dying in the goriest way possible lately?" Jablonsky picked up a glass resting on the end table. "This smells like wine."

Bobby pointed at the open bottle sitting on the side bar table in the corner. "Probably from that bottle there. Do we have a uniform talking to the doorman? A place like this has to have someone to keep the riff-raff from coming in."

"Yeah. Hansen and his partner are on it. We have other detectives going door-to-door in the building to see if anyone heard anything. Have a guess when she might have been killed."

"The fact that the blood is still wet, it couldn't have been any earlier than last night some time." Bobby rested his hip on the mahogany desk at one end of the living room and stared down at the beautifully decorated egg set in the middle of the blotter. "How much do you think this thing's worth?"

He reached out to poke it with his finger.

"Don't touch it, Marks." The lieutenant stalked in, her face set in hard lines. "What do we know?"

Bobby shot to his feet and shoved his hands in his pockets like he used to when he went to the store with his mother. "Not much. The lab guys are collecting evidence right now. As soon as we can move the body, I'll take a closer look at the wound."

"What's your gut telling you, Marks?" She pinned him with her fierce light blue eyes.

"It looks like the same M.O. Less blood, but that's because there's only one body."

She clasped her hands behind her back and paced. "How can we have the same M.O. if Thompson was killed? There wasn't any evidence supporting a second killer."

Jablonsky shuffled his feet. "No, ma'am. Marks could be wrong. Miss Vanderlist could have slit her own throat or it could have been a robbery gone wrong."

The lieutenant shot his partner a quelling look, but Bobby wasn't paying attention to them anymore. Libby stood in the archway, motioning him over. When he got to her side, a gurney with a black body bag came to a halt in front of him. The man who pushed it there grabbed the zipper and opened the bag enough for Bobby to take a close look at Mavis's throat.

"Damn," Bobby whispered, his glove-covered fingers hovering over the teeth marks in Mavis's flesh where her jugular had been slashed. "Did you get up-close pictures of those marks?"

Libby shook her head. "I couldn't get close enough, and I need better lighting. I'll get some at the morgue before and after she's cleaned up."

"Thanks. Email them to me as soon as you can."

"Yes, sir." This time Libby's tone wasn't a smart-ass one.

"Good girl." Bobby patted her shoulder and let them take Mavis out of the apartment.

"Well?" The lieutenant gestured for him to join her and Jablonsky in a huddle as far away from the other cops as they could get and not leave the apartment.

"Teeth marks, Lieutenant. Her throat was sliced down to the bone, and I don't think it was a lucky strike, either. The killer knew right where to get her for maximum loss and the quickest access to the blood. I assume he drank it while she lay dying."

"He?" Jablonsky glared at him. "Are you holding out on me?"

Bobby sighed. "No. I just don't see a woman having the strength to slice a person's neck to the bone. You have to have a lot of power to be able to get your knife through all that flesh." He looked at his lieutenant. "No offence meant, Lieutenant."

She shook her head. "You're right, Marks. We'll know more when the M.E. gets through examining the body. I'm not happy about there being another killer running around New York, drinking people's blood."

He fought the urge to drop his gaze and kick at the carpet under his feet like a kid called in front of the Mother Superior at Catholic school. "I'm working on some leads, Lieutenant."

"I know you are, Marks. One of which is on its way to the Smithsonian as we speak. I hope your expert knows what he's doing, or you'll be busted down to beat cop again."

"Yes, ma'am. I have some more information as well."

Her phone rang and she checked the display. "The Commissioner, and only because he probably dialled his phone faster. We'll meet in my office tomorrow morning at eight, and you can fill me in then."

As she walked away, they heard her answer the phone. "We don't know anything yet, sir."

"Who gets to stay here tonight until they're done?" Jablonsky twirled a quarter between his fingers and grinned at Bobby.

"You do. I let you off the Thompson scene because Wendy was sick. I have someone waiting at home for me, and I would prefer not to make them angry, considering it's our first date."

Jablonsky paled a little, but bravely continued, "Finally get lucky, huh? It's been a while."

"Yes, which is why I won't bore you with the details, and you will be that awesome partner I know you are, and cut me loose."

Flipping him the finger, Jablonsky said, "Get out of here. When I see you tomorrow, you better be smiling."

"I plan on it. Thanks." Bobby clapped his partner on the shoulder and left, dropping his booties and gloves into a bag outside the apartment door.

* * * *

Jiggling the key in the lock, Bobby swore quietly. His hands shook, and he couldn't help but laugh. Anyone watching him would think he was drunk or something because he couldn't get his door to unlock.

"Slow down," he muttered and braced his head against the wood. "Nik's still here. He would've called if he was heading home."

Suddenly the door jerked away from him and he tumbled into his apartment, taking out Nik who stood, holding the door. Bobby had enough presence of mind to flip positions, so he landed on his back and cushioned Nik's fall.

"Hey, honey, I'm home," he whispered before slipping a hand to the back of Nik's head and bringing their mouths together.

Someone whimpered and Bobby didn't care if it was him. He drowned in the warm moisture of Nik's mouth, sucking on his tongue, and biting his bottom lip. Nik didn't fight him, just pressed tighter, so their bodies touched from knees to chest, and their groins were aligned perfectly.

Letting go of Nik's head, Bobby slid his hands down to grasp Nik's ass and rocked the man's lower body into his. Nik braced his hands on Bobby's chest and pushed up, straddling his hips and rocking back on Bobby's cock.

Voices from the corridor caught their attention and they froze.

"Shit, the door."

Nik shot to his feet and slammed the door shut, locking it before turning to look at Bobby. After standing, Bobby held out his hand.

"We need to take this into the bedroom. More comfortable and the supplies are closer."

Bobby led a blushing Nik into the bedroom where he waved the man towards the bed. "Strip."

"What about you?" Nik asked, hands already pushing buttons through holes.

"I'm right with you, honey." He winked while he unhooked his gun and badge, placing them on the dresser along with his phone, watch, and keys.

Clothes flew around the room as they got naked, Bobby not even caring where his suit wound up. He had another clean one for tomorrow. Within minutes, Nik sprawled on the bed and Bobby settled between the man's thighs, spreading them a little more to fit his shoulders.

"What about the sixty-nine we were going to enjoy earlier?" Nik trailed his hand over Bobby's head and tugged on his ear lobe.

"I won't say no to it at some other point in time, but right now, I want to bury my cock as deep inside you as I can get."

Nik blinked those big green eyes and Bobby grinned.

"You might want to set your glasses on the night stand there." He pointed at the one to Nik's left. "While you're at it, you also might want to dig out the rubbers and lube."

"What are you going to be doing while I'm scrambling around your drawers?"

Bobby licked from the base of Nik's cock to the flared head and hummed at the salty sweaty taste exploding on his tongue. "I'm going to be busy."

"M-m-m…"

Nik couldn't seem to articulate whatever he wanted to say, and that was how Bobby wanted it. The only thing he wanted Nik to say was his name at the top of his lungs as Bobby fucked him.

Nik reached for the drawer and Bobby let him roll to his side for an easier stretch. He nibbled along the swell of Nik's ass while trailing his fingers down Nik's crease, pausing to rub them over the hole. His lover's breathing stuttered and Nik pushed back, begging with his gorgeous body for more.

"Here." Nik held a foil package and a tube out to him.

He set them to the side after taking them. Placing his hand in the middle of Nik's back, Bobby pushed his man onto his stomach. He grabbed a pillow from beside Nik and stuffed it under the guy's hips.

"Stay like this," he ordered before placing a kiss at the small of Nik's back.

"O-okay." Nik didn't sound sure.

"Trust me. You'll like this."

Bobby never made a promise he couldn't keep.

He grasped Nik's ass cheeks and spread them apart, staring down at Nik's pink pucker. He leant forward and blew a puff of air over the spot.

"Oh wow." Nik arched his back.

"It gets better."

He caressed the soft skin behind Nik's balls with his tongue and continued up, paying close attention to Nik's soft cries as he played with the younger man's ass. Pointing his tongue, he eased it in past the ring of muscles as Nik shoved back into his face.

Once Nik was nice and wet, Bobby pressed his thumb inside, doing his best to stretch his lover's opening. Reaching to the side, he searched for the lube, not stopping or losing contact with the pale body in front of him. He found the lube and popped the top.

"This might be a little cold," he warned before he dripped some down Nik's crease where it caught on his fingers. After he thought he had enough, he set the slick aside.

As Nik gasped, goose-bumps rose along Nik's spine. Bobby pushed the lube into Nik's channel and slid his fingers in as far as he could, twisting them until Nik jumped.

"Got it."

Bobby grinned and let Nik fuck himself while he fumbled with the foil package of the condom. Tearing it open with his teeth, he inched his fingers out.

"No," Nik protested, reaching behind him to grab Bobby's wrist.

He stroked his hand over Nik's shoulder while he managed to roll the rubber down on his own cock one-handed. "Don't worry. I'm just getting ready for you."

Grabbing the lube again, he squirted more onto his cock and tossed the tube on the floor. He spread it around before he placed the crown of his cock at Nik's opening and slowly breached the still tight ring of muscle.

"Bobby." Nik breathed out and relaxed, allowing Bobby to slide even farther in.

"Christ, you're tight." Bobby gripped Nik's hips and shoved until he was balls deep.

He froze and ran his hands over Nik's back, easing the tension he saw and felt in his lover's body. He waited until Nik clenched his inner passage around his shaft before he moved again.

"Are you ready?"

Nik nodded and, with that signal of consent, Bobby started fucking. He pulled out until only the head of his cock remained inside, then slammed back in, hitting Nik's gland with each thrust.

Grunts and pants filled the air along with the smell of sex and sweat. Nik surged up on his knees, forcing Bobby to wrap one arm around Nik's chest to steady him as they moved together, hips grinding and bodies slapping as skin met skin.

Bobby sucked on Nik's shoulder, enjoying the salty taste. He reached down with his other hand and fisted Nik's cock, pumping in rhythm with his own movements. Pre-cum coated his flesh and Nik's shaft, lessening the friction and building the pleasure.

"Oh, Bobby. I'm gonna…"

"I know, Nik. I'm right with you."

He tightened his grip on Nik's cock, demanding his lover's climax. Nik's channel clenched like a vice around Bobby's cock, drawing a shout from him. Liquid heat poured over his hand and he drove into Nik's ass, freezing as he filled his condom.

They slumped to the bed, Bobby keeping his arms around Nik, holding him tight to his chest. He placed his forehead on Nik's back and rested until his breathing slowed.

Nik moaned while Bobby's limp cock slid out. When Bobby had control over his muscles again, he rolled off the bed and went to the bathroom to take care of the condom. He cleaned off his hands and brushed his teeth before taking another wet cloth into the bedroom with him.

He washed Nik gently and tossed the wash cloth in the direction of the bathroom before climbing back into bed. Setting his alarm clock, he thought about how quiet Nik was being.

"Are you okay?" He leant over Nik, bracing himself on his elbow, and brushed the dark curls off Nik's forehead.

A sleepy smile crossed Nik's face as he nodded. "I never felt better, but I should probably get home. I have papers to grade."

"I'm not going to let you go home this late at night. What time is your first class tomorrow?" He laid down next to Nik, resting his arm over the man's stomach.

"Not until eleven, but like I said, I have papers that need to be graded beforehand." Nik didn't seem in a rush to leave, no matter what he said.

"I have to be at the precinct by eight tomorrow morning to brief my lieutenant. You'll be back at your house early enough to either grade them then, or clean up, change your clothes, and head to the university." He buried his face in Nik's sweat drenched curls. "I promise."

"Okay." Nik snuggled closer, pressing his hand to Bobby's heart.

Bobby smiled as he fell asleep, lulled by his lover's soft snores.

Chapter Eight

Nik raced back to his office after class. "Did he call?"

Sheila glanced over the top of her glasses. "Did who call?"

"George, uh, Professor Lattimer."

Sheila flipped through the pink slips in her hand. "Yes. Almost two hours ago." She handed Nik his messages and started to go back to work. "Oh, and that cute detective's called a couple of times as well."

Nik winked at Sheila. "He is pretty hunky, isn't he?"

Sheila fanned her fifty-something year old face. "If I were thirty years younger and twenty pounds lighter, I'd be all over that."

"And a man." Nik winked again as he entered his office.

"All the good ones..." Sheila's voice trailed off as Nik shut his door.

He found Professor Lattimer's phone message and called him.

"It's about time you got back to me," George said, answering the phone.

"Sorry, sir, I was in class. Did you find out anything?"

"Well, the cask is definitely as old as you thought it was. The Knights of Paiderastia crest on the seal is quite interesting."

"How so?"

"Because The Knights of Paiderastia never died out. They took refuge in the background for centuries, but there has been a lot of speculation lately that there's a resurgence."

"How do you know this?"

The professor was silent for a moment. "I have friends. The important thing is, there has to be a reason this cask is showing up now after over five hundred years."

"I still haven't been able to wrap my mind around the cask itself. After all these years how can it be so perfectly preserved and still contain wine? The wine has to be horrible, so why drink it?"

"Wine? You didn't tell me they'd found wine in the cask. Where's it now?"

Nik scratched his head. If he told the professor what he knew, would it get Bobby in trouble? At the same time, the professor had connections Nik had no hope of tapping into. "The bottle was empty when the police found it, but there were clues that it had been recently consumed. They should get the lab results from the residue back anytime."

Once again, the professor went silent.

"Sir, there's something else. I believe there's another crest imbedded in the seal under the one of The Knights of Paiderastia."

"Yes. That was the second reason I called. I believe it is Radu cel Frumos' personal crest."

Nik nodded before realising the professor couldn't see him. "It doesn't surprise me. Radu was one of the most powerful supporters of the Paiderastians. So you think this cask was made for him?"

"I do."

The tone in the professor's voice, had goose-bumps breaking out on Nik's skin. "Is there something you're not telling me?"

"I need to do more research, but I don't think you should get mixed up in this. Why don't you let me deal directly with the NYPD."

"That's okay, professor. I'd appreciate it if you'd continue to call me with your findings."

"This could get very dangerous. I'm advising you to drop it now."

Nik ran a hand over the prickling hair on the back of his neck. He had no doubt the professor was keeping something from him. "Professor Lattimer? You'd tell me if you knew something else, right?"

Silence. "I'll be in touch, Nikolay."

The phone went dead, and Nik was left wondering what the hell was going on. He pulled out his cell phone and called Bobby.

"Hey," Bobby answered, sounding harried.

"Hi. I just got off the phone with Professor Lattimer. He confirmed the age of the cask, The Knights of Paiderastia crest and the Radu cel Frumos crest."

"That's good, right?"

"Yes and no. There's something he's not telling me. I'm going to go back over to the library and do some research."

"Call me when you're done. If I'm off, I'll pick you up."

"Okay." Bobby's voice had gone a long way in soothing Nik's nerves, but he knew the detective was busy now that he had another murder on his hands. "Guess I'll see you later."

"Is there something wrong, Nik?"

"Just on edge, I guess. I'll talk to you later."

"Call me if you need me."

"Thanks. I will." Nik hung up and stuffed the phone in his backpack along with the pictures of the crest and cask. He slung the pack over his shoulder and turned off his lights. "I'm leaving for the day, Sheila."

The secretary glanced up. "You look white as a ghost. Are you sick?"

Thinking fast, Nik nodded. "I might need you to cancel my classes for a couple of days. I'll give you a call when I know for sure."

"Go home and take care of yourself, and for god's sake, don't breathe on me."

Nik grinned and walked out of the office. He needed to learn everything there was to know about Radu cel Frumos and the Paiderastians.

* * * *

Once in the reference section, Nik stepped up to the large desk. "Is Edna Grant working?"

"Yes. I believe she's in our manuscripts and archives division." The woman pointed in the direction.

"Thanks. I know where it is." He looked at the scrap of paper in his hand. According to the computer on the main level, the library housed several items on The Knights of Paiderastia. It didn't give a location for the items, instead requesting the researcher contact a librarian for assistance. Hopefully Edna would be able to help him find them.

After searching the room, he finally spotted the elderly woman he'd spoken to a few days prior. "Ms. Grant?"

Edna jumped and turned around. "Yes. Professor Radin, isn't it?"

"Yes, ma'am." He held out the sheet of paper. "I was wondering if you could help me find these."

An expression crossed Edna's face that Nik couldn't read. Without another word, she led him through a series of shelves to a locked room. She used her key to open the door and turned on the lights. Instead of normal florescent, the light fixtures were outfitted with black light bulbs. It was his first clue how old the documents he'd asked for were.

Edna gestured towards a small desk. "Wait here while I get them."

While he waited, Nik opened his backpack and took out his notebook and the pictures Bobby had given him. It was several minutes before Edna returned with two, thin boxes. She set them on the desk in front of Nik and handed him a pair of nitrate gloves.

Edna handed Nik back the slip of paper and pointed towards the last item. "We don't have this one. It disappeared from the archives many years ago."

Nik tucked the nugget of information away for later. "Thank you."

He expected Ms. Grant to leave, but instead she took a seat beside the door. Nik didn't take it personally. Evidently, the library wasn't taking chances with more of their precious material walking out.

Nik hoped he'd find something worth all the trouble.

* * * *

"Thanks again." Nik gave Edna a final wave before heading upstairs. He pulled the cell phone out of his pack and called Bobby.

"You finished?" Bobby asked upon answering.

"For now. I'll be back though. I've come away with a lot more questions than I had when I went in. Are you in the area?"

"Not far. I should be there in ten minutes or so. I've got a late meeting with Mavis Vanderlist's mother and father."

Nik walked out of the library and sat on the steps about half-way down. "Then don't worry about me. Go ahead and do what needs doing. I'll catch the bus home. You can call when you're done."

"I just don't like the idea of you taking a bus."

Nik rolled his eyes. He stood and started down the steps towards the bus stop. "I've gotten around this city on public transportation since I was a child. Since when are you so paranoid?"

"Since people started showing up dead and someone I like is walking around the city riding buses."

Nik smiled. The cold effects of the disturbing information he'd been deep into all afternoon began to fall away. "Thanks for the concern. I like you, too. But I'll be fine, promise."

"So'd you find out anything you can tell me over the phone?"

Nik set his pack on the bench and dug out his pass. "I found a couple of things on the Paiderastians, but according to the librarian, the one book I really wanted had been stolen years ago."

"Yeah? What book was that?"

"It wasn't really a book, more like a journal. According to the computer, it was rumoured to be written by the great-great grandson of one of Radu's most trusted servants."

"Sounds like quite a coincidence that everything seems to be pointing to this Radu guy, and the one piece of evidence that might confirm it has gone missing."

"That's what I thought, too, but Edna said the journal has been missing for years." The bus pulled up in a whine of airbrakes and Nik stepped up and swiped his pass. "Most of the research I found dealt with the Paiderastians, so I'm going to keep on that for the time being."

"Why? Something interesting?"

"I think so. Professor Lattimer advised me to step away from the case. I think he knows something about The Knights of Paiderastia that he's not sharing. He did tell me the society is once again on the rise."

"But he didn't explain why he thinks you should step away?" Bobby asked.

"Nope. That's what's bothering me. I don't know how to explain it, but there was something in the way he said it that made the hair on the back of my neck stand up."

"Does he think your digging will endanger you?"

Nik glanced out of the window. He could tell from Bobby's tone he was starting to worry his new lover. It would be just like Bobby to side with Professor Lattimer if he thought Nik was in danger. But he was too far into this thing to stop now. "I don't know. I doubt it. I think it was more of a general warning. Hell, maybe he just wants the glory for himself."

"Is he that kind of man?"

Nik thought about all he knew of his old professor. Even while teaching, George Lattimer had connections. When he'd student taught for the man, Nik had even overheard a short phone conversation between the professor and the

Secretary of State. Nik assumed Professor Lattimer used those connections to get his job at the Smithsonian.

"Nik?"

"Sorry. No. To answer your question, I don't think he's that kind of man. First of all, he doesn't even know what case we're working on, and secondly, he doesn't need the NYPD's help in advancing his career."

Even though he didn't tell Bobby, Nik did feel the professor had an ulterior motive for wanting Nik off the case. He shook his head and rolled his eyes. He was beginning to think of himself as a detective instead of a freaking geek. "Listen, my transfer's coming up, so I'll let you go. Call me later?"

"You bet. Why don't you give me a call when you get home to let me know you made it? If I'm already in my meeting, just leave a voicemail."

"Okay. Bye."

"Bye, babe."

Nik smiled at the endearment as he got off the bus to wait for the one that would take him to Chelsea.

It was another twenty-five minutes before he stepped off the bus, six blocks from his townhouse. He was so deep in thought, he didn't hear the footsteps behind him until he was almost at his door.

Nik stopped suddenly and started to turn when something struck him on the back of the head. He went down like a ton of bricks. He was out cold before his face ever hit the steps.

* * * *

"Shit. The door knocker on this place is worth more than my entire house," Jablonsky mumbled as they approached the massive front door of the Vanderlist mansion.

Bobby didn't comment, but he wouldn't have been surprised if his partner wasn't right. The Vanderlists were old New York Dutch money. Mr. Vanderlist's ancestors came to New York when it was still New Amsterdam and managed to amass a fortune that subsequent generations increased.

He rang the doorbell, observing the drawn curtains over all the windows on ground level. He nudged Jablonsky and nodded. "You think the press has been hounding them?"

"I wouldn't doubt it. We suppressed as much information as we could, but just how bloody the crime scene was got leaked." Jablonsky scowled. "I hate leaks. All they think about is the money. They never think about how it might affect a murder investigation."

Before Bobby could do more than grunt, the door swung open and a black-clad woman stared at them from the entrance.

"How may I help you?"

"I'm Detective Marks and this is my partner, Detective Jablonsky. We have an appointment to speak with Mr. and Mrs. Vanderlist."

Bobby flashed his badge at the woman who eyed him like he was the Anti-Christ come to life.

"Follow me. Mrs. Vanderlist is indisposed. Mr. Vanderlist will meet with you in his study."

Was Mrs. Vanderlist playing the role of grieving mother? Or had they been close? Bobby made a mental note to find out.

They walked through the wide reception hall across a marble floor. Wealth screamed from every object in that room, causing Bobby to tuck his hands in his pockets. Breaking something wasn't an option. Hell, he'd have to work until he died to pay Vanderlist back.

The woman knocked on a door and stuck her head around the edge, saying, "The detectives are here, sir."

"Show them in, Luisa."

She pushed the door open wider before turning to gesture to them. "You may go in."

"Thank you."

If Luisa wasn't such a well-trained servant, Bobby bet she would have rolled her eyes at him, but she merely nodded and disappeared back down the hall.

"Detective Marks. Detective Jablonsky. Please come in and sit down. I regret that my wife has taken the news of Mavis's death very hard. They had their disagreements over the years, but a mother loves her daughter."

Vanderlist was dressed in jeans and a light sweater, yet his belief in his superior bloodline showed through in the slight curl of his lip as he shook Bobby's hand. He hated people who assumed that, because they were rich, they were better than anyone else. He shook the man's hand and stepped back, letting Jablonsky take the lead on questioning Vanderlist. His partner didn't let arrogance and other irritating personality traits bother him. Which could explain why he and Bobby had lasted so long as partners.

"Mr. Vanderlist, we're sorry to have to bother you at such a difficult time, but we just have a few questions to ask." Jablonsky shook the man's hand with proper diffidence.

"I understand. The police must do their job. Both the mayor and the commissioner have given me their word that you'll do all you can to find out who murdered my daughter." Vanderlist motioned to two chairs placed in front of a stone fireplace.

Jablonsky shot Bobby a glance. Bobby nodded slightly, giving his partner permission to ask away. He'd wander around the study, see if there might be any clues lying around. Not that he thought there would be. Mavis hadn't been murdered at the house, but he couldn't pass up the opportunity.

"We are doing our best, sir."

Vanderlist strolled over to the side bar, and poured a glass of burgundy liquid. Bobby tensed and the man must have noticed.

"I find a glass of merlot soothes my nerves. Would either of you like something to drink?"

"No, sir. We're on duty." Jablonsky settled into one of the chairs and pulled out his notebook. After flipping to a clean page, he slipped a pencil from his shirt pocket. "When was the last time you saw your daughter, sir?"

God, Vanderlist was eating up the 'sir' shit. Bobby wanted to gag. He moved over to Vanderlist's desk, resting a hip on the edge. Vanderlist frowned, but didn't stop Bobby.

"Sir, your daughter," Jablonsky prodded.

"Right. I saw her Friday night. We all went to the opera together, then on to dinner. She left us around midnight. My wife and I came home while Mavis went on to one of *those* clubs she likes to visit."

"What kind of clubs would that be?"

Bobby leant back slightly, trying to read the papers on the desk. It looked like Vanderlist was going over some accounts. Probably re-working his will. A stray thought crossed Bobby's mind. Where would all the Vanderlist millions go now that his only heir was dead?

"Mavis enjoyed having a variety of friends. Some of them liked to spend time in Greenwich Village." Disapproval dripped from Vanderlist's voice.

Bobby did roll his eyes at that, but Jablonsky kept a straight face.

"So Miss Vanderlist went to a club in the Village. Do you know the name?"

Vanderlist glared at Jablonsky. "I'm sure I have no idea."

Straightening, Bobby paused when Vanderlist looked at him. "Maybe you could give us the names of some of your daughter's friends. We'll need to talk to them."

"Certainly. I'll have Luisa retrieve Mavis's address book." Vanderlist stood and walked around the desk to the phone.

"I thought your daughter lived in the apartment where we found her." Jablonsky shuffled through his pages.

"That was where she took her men. I told her she couldn't bring them here. It was disrespectful to her mother and me." Vanderlist punched the intercom button. "Luisa, will you bring Mavis's address book to the study?"

"Yes, sir."

Vanderlist opened a drawer and removed a box. The intricately carved top caught Bobby's attention. There was something familiar about it. Vanderlist retrieved a cigar from the box, clipped off one end, and lit it while they waited for Luisa to bring the book.

Jablonsky studied the rug under his feet, and Bobby itched to get a closer look at the cigar box. Vanderlist snatched up his empty glass and went back to pour himself more wine. Bobby edged over to the corner where the box sat.

Luisa entered and Vanderlist took the address book before dismissing her. Bobby glanced at the engraving on the top of the mahogany square. Excitement shot through him. He had seen that seal somewhere before recently.

Shooting a look over his shoulder, he spotted Vanderlist talking to Jablonsky. Bobby tugged out his phone and snapped a quick photo of it. The lab guys could probably enhance it.

An envelope symbol flashed on his screen. He scrolled through his missed calls to see that Nik had called him a few minutes earlier. For some reason, an odd wave of uneasiness swelled over him. Bobby shook himself. He was overreacting simply because he didn't like the idea of Nik riding public transportation. He'd seen and heard too many bad things that had happened to people who rode the buses or subways.

"Certainly, Mr. Vanderlist. We'll keep you informed and get this back to you as soon as possible." Jablonsky raised his voice a little to draw Bobby back to him.

"Thank you, Detective. My wife and I will be happy to cooperate in any way you need us." Vanderlist led the way back to the front door.

As soon as the door closed behind them, Jablonsky turned to Bobby. "What did you find on his desk that you had to take a picture of?"

"Shit. Did he realise what I was doing?"

Jablonsky shook his head. "Not that I know of. I distracted him until I was sure you were done."

Bobby called the picture up on the screen of his phone. "Vanderlist's cigar box has this engraving on it. I'm pretty sure this is the same seal that was on the cask we found at Thompson's house."

"Are you serious?" His partner poked him. "This could be what we're looking for."

"I need to have Nik look at it and verify what I think it is. If I'm right, we might have our connection between the murders and a good suspect."

They climbed into their car. It was Jablonsky's turn to drive, so Bobby listened to his voicemail while Jablonsky pulled into traffic.

"Hey, Bobby. It's Nik."

Bobby frowned. Nik didn't sound good.

"Um-m-m…I know you said to call you when I got home, but I wanted to let you know that I'm not home yet. I'm in the emergency room at Beth Israel. I think I was mugged."

"Fuck." Bobby ended the call and slammed his fist against his thigh.

"What's wrong?"

Bobby scrubbed his hand over his face and repeated what he'd heard. "I knew I should have given him a ride home instead of letting him take the bus."

"Don't worry. I'll get you there asap." Jablonsky turned on the siren and lights.

His partner would do all he could to get them to the hospital, but it wouldn't be fast enough for Bobby.

* * * *

Bobby rushed up to the check-in desk after Jablonsky brought the car to a stop outside the ER. The nurse looked up, ready to yell, but he flashed his badge.

"I'm Detective Marks. I was informed that a Professor Nikolay Radin was brought in thirty minutes ago."

She typed some stuff in the computer and nodded. "Yes, he was, Detective. I'll buzz you in and have a nurse take you to his room."

"Thank you."

"Hey, Bobby, do you want me to stick around?" Jablonsky stopped him.

"No. I'll take him home with me in a cab. Thanks. I'll call you when we get there. Let you know how he's doing." He slapped his partner on the shoulder.

"Okay, man. I'll let the lieutenant know what we found out from the parents. Also, I'll start calling the victim's friends."

"I owe you."

"Don't worry. I'll collect at some point." Jablonsky waved him away as a nurse came for him.

"How is he?" Bobby asked the nurse as she led him back to Nik's room.

"He'll be fine, but I'll let the professor tell you himself." After showing Bobby to Nik's curtained off area, she turned and walked away.

His heart dropped as Nik looked up when he walked in. A bandage marred his lover's right cheek, along with one on the back of his head. Bobby rushed to the side of the bed and clasped Nik's hand in his.

"Are you okay?"

Nik drew a shaking breath and nodded, wincing. "I am now."

He slid his hand around the back of Nik's head, careful not to touch the bandage. Leaning forward, he brushed a kiss over Nik's trembling lips. He demanded entrance and swept in when Nik opened for him. Bobby was shaken by how afraid he'd been since the instant he heard Nik's voice on the phone. Tasting Nik eased him a little, but his nerves wouldn't completely settle until he could hold Nik in his arms and check for himself that he wasn't injured worse than he imagined.

Easing away, he looked down into Nik's eyes and asked, "What happened?"

Uncertainty shaded Nik's eyes. "I'm not sure. I got off the bus and walked to my house. I heard footsteps coming up behind me. I turned to see who it was. Then there was this flaring pain at the back of my head...and I don't remember anything else."

"I should have driven you home from the library." Guilt soured his stomach.

Nik cradled his face and gave him a brief smile. "It's not your fault. I told you not to worry about me."

They broke apart as the doctor came in. Bobby listened closely to all the instructions.

"Now, Professor Radin, do you have someone who can stay with you? I don't want you left alone tonight."

"He'll be staying with me, Doctor." Bobby met Nik's gaze, daring the man to protest.

Nik didn't say anything, and the doctor looked happy.

"Then I'll sign the release forms. The stitches will need to be taken out in two weeks, but you can go to your regular doctor for that." The doctor flipped through some papers on the chart. "I'll send a nurse in with a wheelchair."

"Thank you, Doctor." He watched the man leave. Turning to Nik, he asked, "Where's your stuff?"

A wild look crossed Nik's face. "Oh no! My backpack is missing. All the research I did today is gone."

"Fuck." Every instinct Bobby had pinged. "You are definitely staying with me then. I don't think this is a normal mugging."

"I'm sorry."

"You don't have anything to be sorry for, Nik. I'm sorry for not realising just how dangerous this case could end up being. I mean, even your old professor told you to back off."

The nurse arrived with a wheelchair, and they left the hospital. As he hailed a cab, Bobby decided he'd get Nik settled and talk to his lieutenant. She'd want to know what happened, plus she should know his relationship with Nik was more than work-related.

Chapter Nine

Nik lay beneath the covers, his hands tucked near his cheek, and there were still black circles under his eyes. Bobby hated having to wake him, but his lieutenant demanded Nik's presence in her office at ten, and Bobby figured it was a good time to catch everyone up on Nik's research.

Sitting on the edge of the bed, he smiled as Nik rolled over and nestled closer to him, resting a hand on Bobby's thigh. He pushed the black curls off Nik's forehead and lightly trailed a finger over the bandage hiding the cut on Nik's cheek. God, he hated the thought of Nik getting hurt, especially since he was the one who brought Nik in on the case.

It wasn't that Bobby didn't think Nik could handle himself in most situations, but this wasn't an ordinary case and…Bobby's gut churned. He'd only known Nik a few days, and already the professor had wormed his way into Bobby's heart. He'd never be able to forgive himself if something worse happened to Nik.

He leant over and brushed a kiss over Nik's lips. Nik murmured, rubbing his face against Bobby's thigh. Bobby shifted and his cock started to fill. His lover wrinkled his nose, and sniffed delicately. He muffled his chuckle and reached under the blankets to stroke down Nik's chest to where a small nipple hardened under his touch.

"Hmmm…" Nik hummed, arching as Bobby pinched his flesh between his thumb and finger.

Checking the clock, Bobby noted that they had a little extra time. He eased down onto the bed, pushing the covers down until Nik's groin was revealed. Nudging Nik's legs apart, he settled between them and kissed along the crease where Nik's hip and thigh met.

"Bobby?" Nik pushed up on his elbows and blinked down at Bobby.

"Who else did you expect in the bed with you?" He grinned before licking from the base of Nik's cock to the tip, pressing his tongue in the slit, and drawing a moan from Nik.

"I-I don't know?"

Nik's voice lifted in a question at the end as he thrust up, trying to get Bobby to take him all the way in. Bobby pressed his hands down on Nik's hips and eased away slightly.

"Don't strain yourself, honey. Let me do the work. I don't want you hurting your head or anything."

Nik ran his hand over Bobby's hair. "Can I touch you?"

"I won't argue with that."

"Maybe I could take care of you while you're enjoying me?"

Bobby chuckled, but shook his head at Nik's hopeful smile.

"I'd love to, but not until your head is better." He placed a quick kiss on Nik's hip. "Don't worry. I won't forget you owe me."

Nik gave a little nod and dropped back down, allowing Bobby to have his way. Bobby turned his attention back to Nik's shaft. He swept long wet trails over the pulsing vein along the underside. Quick little tastes teased the soft spongy head and crown. Pre-cum pooled at Nik's slit and Bobby sipped like it was the finest wine.

He slipped one of Nik's legs over his shoulder, giving him better access to Nik's balls. After nuzzling them and breathing in Nik's musky scent, Bobby sucked one into his mouth, bathing it with his tongue.

Bobby grunted as Nik entwined his fingers in his hair and tugged, jerking as Bobby let one ball pop out and took the other one in, not wanting it to feel neglected. He slid his fingers down behind Nik's balls, caressing the soft skin. Nik shuddered.

"Oh my." Nik's breathing hitched as Bobby rubbed his fingers over Nik's rosebud, playing with the nerve-endings hidden there.

Wetting his fingers, Bobby pressed one into Nik's hole while he swallowed Nik's cock down to the root.

"Bobby," Nik shouted, rolling his head from side to side, hands grasping Bobby.

Bobby hummed his approval, bobbing his head up and down. He made sure he kept the suction hard and solid, letting his teeth scrape along the sensitive flesh. Two of his fingers slid into Nik's ass, filling his lover. Twisting his fingers, he managed to hit Nik's gland.

"God."

Nik rocked between Bobby's mouth and fingers. Bobby drove his lover higher and harder, demanding Nik give him everything.

"I'm gonna…"

Warm salty-bitter liquid flooded Bobby's mouth as Nik stopped talking and started coming. He plunged his fingers deep, moaning around Nik's cock as the man's inner muscles clenched around him like a vice.

Every bit of tension disappeared from Nik's muscles. The man lay on the bed like a limp noodle. Bobby licked him clean before climbing out of bed and heading to the bathroom.

"What about you?" Nik waved a hand in his direction.

He shot a glance over his shoulder as he cleaned his hands and brushed his teeth. After wetting a cloth, he returned to wipe Nik down.

"Don't worry about me." He stripped and tossed his soiled underwear and pants at his laundry basket. "You're so dead sexy. I came when you did."

Nik blushed and sat up. "What do we do now?"

"Now, you go grab a shower and get dressed. My lieutenant has requested your presence in her office this morning." He pulled a new pair of pants out of his closet and tugged them on.

"Am I in trouble?" Nik shot out of bed and practically raced towards the bathroom.

"In trouble? Why would you be in trouble?" Bobby frowned as he checked his shirt and tie in the mirror, making sure they weren't too wrinkled.

"Because I lost that research yesterday."

Nik leant over to turn the water on. Bobby couldn't resist reaching out and pinching one of those firm cheeks.

Nik squeaked and whirled around, losing his balance, but grabbing the towel rack just in time to steady himself.

"Watch it, honey. I shouldn't have done that. Forgot about your head." His fingers lingered inches above the wound on the back of Nik's head.

"It's okay." Nik waved Bobby's concern away, seemingly more worried about the lieutenant than his wounds. "Is she mad at me?"

Bobby shook his head. "No, I think she's more upset that you were injured. Her anger is focused on me because I involved you. The lieutenant doesn't like it when civilians get hurt in the course of an investigation."

"I'm sorry."

"Quit apologising. You didn't ask to be attacked or deliberately entice someone to hurt you. The only thing you did was your job. It's not your fault or mine for that matter that there's a crazy person out there who will do whatever he can to keep his crimes hidden."

He snatched up his suit coat from where he'd draped it over the chair.

"Take a shower and get dressed, but don't get your stitches wet. I'll make us some coffee and breakfast. Do you like pancakes?"

He caught the nod Nik sent him before the man stepped into the shower.

The coffee brewed while Bobby whipped up some pancakes and sausage. He couldn't remember the last time he'd made breakfast before going into the precinct. Usually he would stop at one of the bakeries and grab a turnover. Yet something told him Nik didn't eat much or often, and he wanted to take care of the professor.

Snorting softly, he poured some batter onto the griddle, careful not to splatter it on the towel he'd tucked into his waistband. Bobby admitted he'd never wanted to take care of any of his lovers before. Oh, he'd liked most of them and maybe even been in love once or twice, but his feelings for Nik were different, and there wasn't time to analyse any of them just then.

The pancakes came out perfect, and he'd just slid them on the plates as Nik joined him in the kitchen. Bobby pulled out a chair and gestured for Nik to sit.

"Here's your coffee. I didn't know how you took it, so there's creamer and sugar on the table."

He got the butter and syrup out along with the strawberry jam one of his elderly neighbours gave him. Everything was on the table and he sat, noticing how Nik studied him.

"What?"

"Do you always eat breakfast like this?" Nik nodded towards the pile of food he'd made.

Bobby's cheeks heated. "Not all the time, but usually it's just me, and I can never make food for just one person. I tend to cook enough for several people as you can see."

"Thank you for taking the time to feed me." Nik stroked his fingers over the top of Bobby's hand.

"You're welcome. Now eat up."

A comfortable silence filled the room while they shared breakfast. Nik insisted on rinsing the plates before stacking them in the dishwasher. Bobby peeked at the clock as they grabbed their stuff and headed out of Bobby's apartment.

He pulled out his phone and punched in a number.

"Jablonsky."

"Hey, partner. We're on our way in." He unlocked the door of his car and held it open for Nik.

"Okay. I'll let the lieutenant know. How's the professor doing?"

Bobby glanced over at Nik as he slid behind the wheel. The cut stood out on Nik's pale skin, and there was a slight grimace of pain quirking the corners of the man's mouth. "He's feeling a little pain, but he took some medicine and should be okay."

"Glad to hear that." A voice murmured in the background. "I have to go, Bobby. I'll see you when you get here."

"Bye."

He closed his phone and set it in the console between him and Nik. The car rumbled to life as he turned the key.

"You can put on the radio if you want." He backed out of his spot and headed to the gate.

Nik tuned the radio to a classical station. Bobby winced, but didn't say anything. He should have known Nik would like the old stuff. Reaching over, he gripped Nik's hand and brought it over to rest on his thigh. Nik twisted in his seat to look at Bobby.

"Do you really think my attack was about your case, and not just a random mugging?"

Bobby thought about it for a moment before he nodded. "They didn't take anything except your backpack. They could have pushed you inside and stole the expensive stuff in your house."

"I don't have any expensive stuff," Nik pointed out.

"You have a computer, right?" At Nik's nod, he said, "There you go. You have things that any mugger could pawn for money. Your attacker didn't. He was looking for something specific, I believe, and it must have been your research."

Nik rubbed his forehead with his free hand. "I'll have to go back to the library and do it all again."

"Well, you're not going anywhere without me." A thought hit him. "Did you call the university and let them know you're not going to be in today?"

"Yes. Sheila said she'd let them know. I should feel good enough tomorrow to go back."

Traffic was rather light, so they got to the precinct with time to spare. Bobby relaxed. The lieutenant hated tardiness, and Bobby had seen how she dealt with tardy detectives.

After parking, they headed inside and up to the homicide floor. Jablonsky waited for them at their desks. Bobby picked up his files on the Thompson and Vanderlist cases.

"Professor Nikolay Radin, this is my partner, Detective Kenneth Jablonsky. Jablonsky, this is our expert witness, Professor Nikolay Radin."

Nik and Jablonsky greeted each other and made small talk until the lieutenant stuck her head out of her office door and gestured to them.

"Showtime," Jablonsky muttered as they wound their way through the maze of desks to where their boss waited.

"Shut the door and close the blinds, gentlemen." The lieutenant motioned to the chairs. She held out her hand to Nik. "Professor Radin, I'm Lieutenant Molly O'Donnell. I want to thank you for all of the work you've been doing on our behalf. I'm sorry you were injured."

Nik blushed, but shook the lieutenant's hand. "Nice to meet you, ma'am."

"Okay, niceties taken care of. I'd like you to bring us up-to-date with what you've discovered in your research."

Bobby nodded towards the chair closest to her desk, letting Nik know he should sit there. Jablonsky took the chair nearest the door, which left Bobby sitting next to Nik.

Nik glanced at Bobby before returning his attention to his lieutenant. "With my research stolen, I can't give you specific dates, but I can give you an overall summary of what I've found so far."

"That's fine." The lieutenant sat back in her chair and smiled, putting Nik at ease.

"Well, we know the seal on the cask is made up of two different crests. The Knights of Paiderastia stamped over Radu cel Frumos personal crest. For this discussion, I think it would be easier to examine the crests separately."

As he began, Nik's fingernail automatically went to the sore patch of skin on his thumb. "The Knights of Paiderastia were once wealthy, powerful men who, according to the texts I've uncovered, found spiritual fulfilment through their love of boys. Ancient Greeks and Romans found the act of pederasty quite acceptable. It was all very civilised at the time. A wealthy man would gain permission from a boy's father to bring him into his household. He'd oversee the educational upbringing of the young man. In some cases, the relationship between the boy and the man was strictly spiritual, in others, sexual."

"Are we talking about paedophilia, Dr. Radin?" the lieutenant asked.

Nik nodded. "In today's legal terms, yes. But once again, it was an accepted practice in Ancient Greece. Through the years, society began to change their minds on the morality of the practice, at one point making pederasty illegal. This appears to be the time frame when The Knights of Paiderastia society formed. Whether or not the men involved still believed in the religious aspects of the practice is unknown."

Nik took a breath. He wasn't sure if he should share the information Professor Lattimer imparted regarding the society, since he had nothing to back it up. "From what I understand, The Knights of Paiderastia are still active, at least in the United States and Europe, my guess is worldwide."

The lieutenant sat up straight and narrowed her eyes. "Go on."

"I've been thinking about the society, and I believe the memberships are passed down between generations. Their existence is too secretive to allow outsiders to join. I think it's the reason most people have never heard of them."

The lieutenant nodded and reached for her cup of coffee. "And the other crest?"

"Radu cel Frumos was the half-brother of Vlad Tepes, also known as Vlad the Impaler, but most importantly, Vlad was the ruler the book Dracula was modelled after. Radu was a member of The Knights of Paiderastia as well as several other powerful men at the time. In his youth, Radu was kept by a sultan at the receiving end of a pederast relationship. Although related, Radu and Vlad Tepes were enemies, especially after the death of their other brother, Mircea, and their father Vlad Dracul II, when Vlad Tepes was granted ruling power over Wallachia."

Nik shut up when he saw he was beginning to lose focus. The lieutenant hadn't asked for a history lesson, he had to remember that. "There's a journal in existence that was written by Radu's young servant's ancestors.

Evidently stories were passed down in the family, and one of them chose to record these stories. The New York Public Library was in possession of the journal until a few years ago when it was stolen from the archives. I believe the journal is the key to understanding what's going on."

"How so?" the lieutenant questioned. "Although we now know the cask originally came from Radu, what would that have to do with the murders happening now?"

Bobby jumped in. "The victims are being drained of their blood. We still don't know why, but we believe it has to be connected to the cask and the history of Radu's relationship with his brother, Vlad the Impaler." Bobby cleared his throat. "We also think The Knights of Paiderastia play a large part in the murders. When I went to question Mr. Vanderlist, I noticed a cigar box on his desk with a sterling silver crest adorning its top. The crest was that of The Knights of Paiderastia."

Lieutenant O'Donnell narrowed her eyes. "You're walking a fine line, Marks. Vanderlist has connections that could have us both walking the beat if we're not careful."

Bobby nodded. "I realise that, Lieutenant, but it's a lead I need to follow. I'd like permission to search Morgan Thompson's house again. If I'm right, we'll find something that links him to the Paiderastians."

The lieutenant tapped her pen on the desk as she considered Bobby's request. "We haven't released the crime scene yet, so access isn't a problem. The political implications should you find something connecting one of the wealthiest men in the city with a society of perverts could be damaging."

Bobby nodded once again. "I understand that, but our job is to find the hows and whys of this case and to bring the whos to justice. We can't do that if we're constantly worried about pissing the rich and powerful off."

"I'd suggest you work quickly before your investigation is jeopardised." Her gaze swung between the three men in the room. "I've got to give the higher ups a full rundown at the end of the day."

Bobby stood, and Nik followed suit. "We'll head over to Thompson's now."

Nik followed Bobby out of the office with Jablonsky bringing up the rear. Once they were back at the side by side desks of the two detectives, Nik spoke. "I want to go with you."

Bobby shook his head. "It's too dangerous."

"I'll have two big cops with me. Besides, I want to look over the books in Thompson's library."

Bobby's brows shot up. "You think Thompson stole the book from the library?"

Nik shrugged. "I don't know, but if he did, I'll find it."

Bobby looked at his partner. "I think we should watch Vanderlist. Even if I hadn't seen the crest, I'd say he knows more than he's willing to tell us. There's something about that man that makes my skin crawl."

Jablonsky stopped in the process of stuffing folders into a briefcase. "I'm guessing you want me to do that."

Bobby nodded. "At least while we're at Thompson's. I'll relieve you later so you can make it home to the family in time for supper."

Jablonsky sighed and rolled his eyes. "I hate stakeouts."

"Don't we all." Bobby clapped his partner on the back. "Call me if you see anything in the least suspicious."

Jablonsky picked up his briefcase and headed out the door.

"You ready?" Bobby asked, turning to Nik.

Nik nodded. "Do you have a camera?"

Bobby rested his hand on his briefcase. "In here along with gloves."

As he followed Bobby to the issued sedan, he reached into his pocket for the small tube of pain relievers, popping two in his mouth.

"You okay?" Bobby rested a hand on the small of Nik's back.

"Just a headache."

Bobby's expression turned to worry. "Maybe it would be better if I took you back to my place while I search Thompson's."

"I'm fine, really. I want to go with you."

Bobby opened the passenger door and Nik got in. He reached across the seat to unlock the driver's door. Once Bobby was behind the wheel, he reached out and threaded his fingers through Nik's.

"I'm worried about letting you get even more involved than you already are."

Nik squeezed his lover's hand. "I know you are, and I'll be careful."

Bobby started the car and pulled out of the garage.

"Can I see that picture of Vanderlist's cigar box again?" Nik asked.

Bobby pulled out his cell and called up the image, before handing the phone to Nik. "I wish the quality was better, but I was in a hurry."

Nik studied the small picture. "It's old. See the rounded corners of the box? I think this is probably something inherited."

Bobby's right eyebrow rose. "It would further your theory of membership being passed down within a family."

Nik nodded. He wondered once again about Professor Lattimer's warnings. Did the professor know a lot more about the society than he was telling Nik? Perhaps it was the reason he'd been warned.

Bobby lifted Nik's hand and kissed it. "Penny for your thoughts?"

He hated to voice his concerns regarding his old friend, but knew he could always apologise later if they turned out to be nothing. "I'm worried about Professor Lattimer's role in this. Not only did he warn me to stay away from further investigating this case, but he's also the one who sent me to see Edna at the library."

"You think the librarian has something to do with it?"

Nik shrugged. "I don't know, but isn't it odd that I was mugged after spending an entire afternoon making notes?"

He noticed Bobby's free hand grip the steering wheel. "You're not going back to the library, that's for sure. I'll have to dig deeper into Lattimer's background."

"Deeper? You mean you've already been investigating him?"

Bobby nodded. "Procedure. We were shipping a stranger a valuable piece of evidence."

"Did anything out of the ordinary come up?" Nik held his breath, waiting for the answer.

"Not really. Other than the fact he's also from 'old money'. His great-grandfather was Peirce Lattimer, founder and co-owner of L & M Bank. Sorry, I figured you knew."

Nik shook his head. "His connections to the rich and famous make a little more sense. I wonder how deep the connections go?" He once again began picking at his tortured thumb. "I'm glad I didn't mention Mavis Vanderlist's death to him."

"One thing I learned a long time ago was to follow your gut. If something's telling you to suspect Lattimer, I'd go with it. Make sure you don't share any more than you absolutely have to."

"Makes sense." Nik closed his eyes and leaned his head carefully against the back of the seat. "What if I've screwed everything up by bringing in Lattimer?"

"I don't think you've screwed anything up, but I do worry about the danger you've put yourself in. If Lattimer isn't on the up and up and he thinks you know more than you do..." Bobby squeezed Nik's hand. "I think you should stick close to me."

Nik agreed. Not only for his own safety, but because he was quickly becoming used to the brawny detective. "After we finish at Thompson's place, would you take me by my house for a change of clothes?"

"I think it would be wise for you to pack a bag. I don't see this investigation wrapping up anytime soon, and, until the danger dies down, I'm not letting you sleep anywhere but with me." Bobby finished the statement with a wink that had Nik's cock twitching in response.

When they pulled up to Morgan Thompson's Manhattan mansion, the first thing Nik noticed was the lack of yellow tape. "I thought the lieutenant said they hadn't released the house?"

"They haven't, but the neighbours were complaining, so they took down everything on the outside of the house except the seal on the door."

Nik spotted a teenager standing at the black iron gate. "Looks like we have company."

Bobby turned off the engine and pocketed the keys. "Stay here while I check him out."

Nik reluctantly agreed, and waited while Bobby approached the young man. They talked for several moments before the boy ran off. Bobby motioned for Nik to get out.

Joining Bobby on the sidewalk, Nik glanced in the direction of the retreating stranger. "Get anything?"

Bobby rubbed the back of his neck. "He just said he knew Morgan and was shocked by the news of his death. He said Morgan was a gentle man and he doubted he'd really done the things Morgan has been accused of."

"How would a boy like that know Thompson? They definitely hadn't run in the same social circles."

Bobby grinned and slit the seal on the door with his pocket knife. "By the emotions evident in the boy's eyes, I'd say they might have run in the same social circles, just not the ones admitted to in public."

The thought of the sweet young boy being involved with The Knights of Paiderastia turned Nik's stomach. He followed Bobby inside the house, wanting more than anything to expose the secret society for the sickos they were.

Chapter Ten

The noise from his cell phone startled him. The particular song he had attached to other members of the brotherhood rarely sounded, especially during the middle of the afternoon.

One glance at the display, and he was worried even more. "Excuse me."

He left the conference room and stepped into his private office. "Yes."

"What's going on? I went by Morgan's house and the police were back. The detective pretty much ran me off, but I went back and looked in the windows. They're in the study, going through Morgan's desk and bookshelves."

The boy was in a near panic. He groaned, knowing he now had two new situations to handle. "Stay calm. They don't know anything."

"Easy for you to say. I need money. I need to get away from here."

He ground his teeth. Phillip Cochran was going to be a problem, one that needed to be taken care of. He stuck his hand in his pocket and ran his fingers over the cold silver of his flask. With the help of his liquid courage, he should be able to accomplish both tasks by the end of the business day.

"Meet me at our regular place at four."

"You'll bring money?"

"Haven't we always taken care of you, Phillip?"

"Yes, sir."

"Be there at four." He snapped his phone shut and stuck his head back into the conference room. "Something's come up that requires my attention. I'll have my secretary call you with the rescheduled time."

With that, he walked out of the building and climbed into his car. He pulled the antique flask from his pocket and drank the sweet wine. Maybe if he was lucky, he'd have the chance to sip from Phillip's sweet young body before killing him.

He took another drink. *Yes, I'll definitely need a proper meal before dinner.* He headed in the direction of Morgan Thompson's to take care of his first problem.

* * * *

As soon as they were in the house, Bobby opened his briefcase and handed Nik a pair of gloves. "I've got evidence bags as well, so holler if you need one."

Nik nodded and pulled on the gloves as he made his way to Thompson's study. The wall of books he'd only seen in the crime scene photos came into view, making him gasp.

"Something wrong?"

Nik's gaze never left the floor to ceiling shelves. "No. I've just never seen a collection quite like this. These books are worth a fortune."

"Well, since I know absolutely nothing about books not written by Tom Clancy or Louis L'Amour, I'm going to check out the desk and leave you to it."

Nik chuckled as he neared the shelves. He knew antique and out-of-print books weren't everyone's cup of tea. That was fine with him. It would give him a chance to thoroughly investigate each and every volume. He decided to start at the top and work his way down. He slid the library ladder to the far corner and climbed up.

He was glad he had gloves on which allowed him to physically touch each and every spine as he read through Thompson's collection. As he worked his way down the row, he couldn't help but whistle. "I hope to hell he willed these to a museum or library."

"That impressive, huh?"

Nik glanced over his shoulder at Bobby. "Thompson must've been into a bit of everything. There are books here that delve into subjects from the rise of Christianity to black magic."

He pulled out a thick leather-bound volume. "This one is spells from an old voodoo priestess." He shook his head. "Fucking amazing."

Bobby closed the drawer he'd been going through. "You think we're dealing with some kind of witchcraft?"

Nik shook his head. "No. I think we're dealing with a man who got off on delving into the underbelly of polite society." He slid the heavy book back into place and continued down the row.

After forty-five minutes, Nik climbed down the ladder. He took off his glasses and unconsciously began to clean them.

"Giving up?"

"No. I just feel like something's off. So far, all the books I've found belonged to Thompson's ancestors. So, where are his?"

Bobby shrugged. He closed the drawer he was digging in and walked over to wrap an arm around Nik. "Maybe he didn't enjoy them like his forefathers did."

Nik shook his head. "With a collection this impressive, Morgan would've felt it was his obligation to continue to add to them."

"I don't understand why you think he hasn't?"

Nik pulled a large book from the shelf and opened it to the first page. "See this?" He pointed towards a small pencilled in date with the initials JAT. "This book was acquired in 1914 by James Allen Thompson, Morgan's great grandfather."

"Aren't you the little smarty pants." In an uncharacteristic move, Bobby laughed and bumped Nik with his hip.

Nik grinned up at his silly lover. "Of course I am, otherwise you wouldn't need me."

Bobby bent and kissed Nik. "I'm beginning to think I'll need you long after this investigation is over."

The statement warmed Nik's heart. He pulled Bobby's head back down for a deeper kiss, sweeping his tongue through the interior of his lover's mouth. He rubbed his growing erection against Bobby's hip and moaned into the kiss, completely forgetting where they were.

Bobby pulled back first, smiling down at Nik. "Let's get this finished so I can take you home."

With a dramatic sigh, Nik broke away and turned back to the shelf. He noticed the empty space from the book he'd pulled earlier and flushed. "Oops. Guess you had me a little distracted."

Bobby leant over and picked the heavy leather bound volume off the floor and handed it back to Nik. "I like being your distraction."

Nik gave Bobby's arm a playful slap. He turned to put the book back in its place and stopped. "Uhhh, Bobby?"

Already on his way back to the desk, Bobby answered over his shoulder. "Yeah, honey?"

Nik pointed towards the shelf. "There looks to be some kind of release lever."

He set the book on the nearest table before turning the small brass handle. He heard a click, but that was it.

"Did it do anything?"

Nik shook his head. "Not yet." He rested both hands on the shelf and pulled, when nothing happened, he pushed. The entire section of the bookcase, from just under the moulding to the floor, swung inwards. "Bingo!"

Nik started to enter the dark room, but Bobby grabbed his hand. "No. Let me get my camera and go in first."

Nik nodded. He'd been so excited by the hidden room, he hadn't even thought of gathering crucial evidence. *Guess that's why I'm not the cop.*

Bobby returned with his briefcase and retrieved the camera and a flashlight. Nik was dutifully impressed. "Wow, that thing's like a clown car."

Chuckling, Bobby snapped on the flashlight and entered the darkened room. After several moments, a light turned on, illuminating the interior. "Holy fuck."

Nik took a chance and poked his head into the room. "Holy fuck is right."

"I guess we know where Morgan Thompson practiced his chosen religion."

The room looked like something out of a porn flick. A large round bed shrouded in white organza sat centre stage. Bobby was busy snapping photographs as Nik eased his way into the room. His gaze shot to the wall of books. "I knew it."

"Wait." Bobby crossed the room and took a handful of shots. "All yours."

Nik stepped forward, cleaning his glasses. He settled them back on his face and ran a gloved hand over one of the spines. "This is more like it."

"Something interesting?" Bobby asked as he continued to snap pictures.

Nik gently removed a book and opened the cover. "Wow. This looks like one of the editions published by Sir Richard Burton in 1883."

"The actor?"

Nik chuckled and rolled his eyes. "No." Nik replaced the book after noting the year, 1973 MAT. "But this one was obtained by Morgan Thompson."

"So I guess Morgan brought his lovers here?"

Nik nodded. "Whether or not he truly believed it, this room would probably be considered as a sanctuary for him to practice his religion."

"Found something," Bobby called from across the room.

Nik moved to Bobby's side. His lover held a cigar box, the same kind that had been in the Vanderlist study. "Okay, so there's definitely a connection between Thompson and Vanderlist. Can you use it?"

"I can sure as hell try. If nothing else, it should be enough to get a warrant to search Vanderlist's house for one of these fancy hidden lairs."

"Open it."

Bobby used a pencil to unlatch the humidor before lifting the lid at the corners with his gloved hands. Nik gasped, his hand covering his mouth. "That's it."

"The journal?"

Nik quickly closed the lid, protecting the ancient journal from the overhead lights. "I need to study this under black light."

Bobby bit his bottom lip and rested his hands on his hips. "What're you asking?"

"Surely Morgan has a lamp around here. The man's a collector of rare antique books."

Bobby threw up his arms and turned around in a circle. "By all means enlighten me. Where am I supposed to find this magic lamp?"

He was about to snap right back at Bobby when a loud noise, coming from the outer room, startled them both. Bobby immediately drew his weapon and motioned for Nik to hide behind a large wardrobe.

Before he scurried off to the corner, he grabbed the humidor and clutched it to his chest. He swallowed around the lump in his throat as Bobby made his way towards the study.

For the first time, Nik was suddenly very aware of just how dangerous Bobby's job could be. The box Bobby had opened so carefully smashed between Nik's arms and chest. He heard the sound of breaking glass followed by a grunt from Bobby.

Without thinking things through, Nik reached into the humidor and pulled out the journal, stuffing it under his shirt in the waistband of his khaki pants. He stepped out from behind the wardrobe, picking his way towards the study, listening. *Come on, Bobby, make some noise.*

Before he reached the hidden doorway, he was hit by the smell of smoke. Nik blinked his eyes as he surged from the windowless room. If he was going to burn alive, it wouldn't be without a fight.

"Bobby!" he screamed, trying to cover his mouth. The entire outer wall of the mansion appeared to be on fire from floor to ceiling.

"Nik, get out of here!"

Nik spotted a blur of movement he assumed was Bobby. "What're you doing?"

"Get out. I'm getting my briefcase."

Knowing he had the journal, Nik shielded his midsection with his arms and tried to find his way towards the hallway. "Come on!" The scream ended in an uncontrollable cough.

Bobby grabbed Nik's upper arm and pulled him towards the front door. "Shit."

The smoke was so thick at the front of the house, they had no choice but to try to find an alternate way out. Nik was forced to release one hand from the journal to pull his shirt up over his mouth and nose. Unlike modern houses, the Thompson mansion was built in the days of large rooms in a maze of twists and turns. He sure as hell hoped Bobby had a better sense of direction than he did.

A whoosh came from the front of the house as fire exploded one of the windows. Never in his life would he forget the sound of the raging fire behind him. Nik feared the sound alone could swallow him alive.

"This way!" Bobby yelled over the roar, pulling Nik into yet another room. They ran into what appeared to be a dining room filled with smoke. The good news was the room appeared to be flame-free.

Before Nik knew what was happening, Bobby threw a dining room chair through a large picture window. "Hurry."

Nik didn't need to be told twice. With the new supply of oxygen coming in through the broken window, the flames appeared to magically appear in the doorway.

With one arm securing the journal, Nik braced his other hand on Bobby's shoulder and climbed onto the window sill. "Give me your briefcase."

Bobby coughed and shook his head. "Just go."

Nik jumped as far from the burning house as he could and rolled out of Bobby's path. He gulped the much needed air as he heard a thud beside him.

"Come on." Bobby grabbed Nik's upper arm and pulled him to his feet.

Sirens wailed in the background, as Nik struggled to stay on his feet long enough to make it across the street. He sat on the sidewalk, hugging the journal to his stomach.

Bobby handed him the briefcase and gave him a quick kiss. "I'll be right back, I'm gonna move the car while there's still something left to move."

"Forget the car."

"And be forced to fill out mountains of paperwork? No thanks." As Bobby started to turn away, Nik saw the blood running down the side of his lover's head.

He jumped up. "You're hurt."

"I'm fine. Stay here." Bobby jogged across the street just as the first police cruiser pulled up.

Nik stared at the burning house across from him. How close had they both come to dying? Was it worth it? He watched as Bobby said something to the policeman before pulling the sedan away from what was left of Thompson's house.

"Are you okay?" A woman in a maid's uniform asked.

Nik assumed she worked at the house he sat in front of. He wanted to scream a big fat no, but nodded. "I'm okay. Thanks."

As the fire trucks arrived on the scene, neighbours seemed to be pulled from their houses to watch the once impressive mansion being consumed by flames. Nik was no fire inspector, but even he could tell some kind of accelerant had to have been used. It seemed the warning Professor Lattimer issued was well deserved.

* * * *

Bobby winced as the EMT poked at the wound on the side of his head. Nik hovered, worry clouding his eyes. Reaching out, Bobby snagged Nik's hand and drew him closer.

"Are you okay?" He wanted to run his hands over Nik's body to reassure himself that his lover was fine.

"The EMTs already checked me out. Aside from a little smoke inhalation, I'm fine."

Nik leant against him and Bobby slipped his arm around Nik's waist, frowning when his hand encountered something square under Nik's shirt.

"You need to sign this release form since you won't go to the hospital like I suggested." The EMT handed Bobby a clipboard and a pen.

"Wait. I thought you said you were fine." Nik eyed him.

"I am fine. I've been hit harder during street football when I was younger." Bobby signed the form and stood, smiling as Nik slid under his arm to support him as they made their way to Bobby's car.

"What the hell happened here, Marks?"

Both of them stiffened when the lieutenant's voice cut through the noise of the police cars and fire engines. He dropped his arm away from Nik and eased a few inches to the side. No point in getting her worked up about him mixing business with pleasure along with the fact that he let someone torch a crime scene while he was in it.

"There was a fire," Nik spoke up.

She stared at him for a second before re-focusing on Bobby. "How the hell did someone manage to start a fire while you were in the house? You didn't hear anything?"

"We were investigating something when I heard a noise."

"What something?"

He glanced around, not wanting to talk about an open case in the midst of all those people, especially a case that had the potential of being extremely explosive.

"Let's go to your car. You look like you should be in the hospital, Detective."

The lieutenant led the way to Bobby's car where she pointed to the driver's seat. "Sit before you fall over."

Nik opened the door for him and he slumped in the seat, resting his pounding head on the steering wheel while organising his thoughts. Thank God he managed to save his briefcase and the camera. Hopefully, Nik grabbed the journal and, along with the pictures of the cigar box, that would be enough of a connection to start investigating Vanderlist.

"We found a secret room."

She raised her eyebrows and he laughed.

"Yeah, I know. There's no way for you to see it now. I took some pictures. It looked like a place he took his lovers. There were books and pictures all over the place."

"I want to see those photographs, but why do I think you have more than just a room?"

He fumbled through his pockets to find his phone. Opening it, he scrolled through the few photos he had on it to find one in particular. Bobby handed the phone to his lieutenant.

"I haven't had time to email it to the tech guys to get it cleaned up, but I took it at Vanderlist's house. It's a cigar box with a seal of the same kind that was found on the cask at Thompson's."

A dawning expression of understanding appeared on Lieutenant O'Donnell's face. "You're accusing…"

"I'm not accusing anyone, Lieutenant, but we found a box in that secret room of Thompson's that looks remarkably like Vanderlist's."

After handing back his phone, she rubbed her forehead with a sigh. "Are we seriously considering accusing one of the richest men in the city of paedophilia and murder?"

"No, but we have to look into every possibility. We can't gloss over a viable suspect simply because he's rich and friends with the mayor. That isn't how justice works."

He ducked his head. Preaching to the choir wasn't smart because he knew the lieutenant wouldn't bury something like this, but he understood she had to walk a careful line.

"What if you're wrong?"

"I don't think I am."

Nik shifted, drawing Bobby's gaze, and he saw the dark shadow under Nik's shirt. He looked back at his lieutenant, hoping she wouldn't notice it. A small voice in the back of his head whispered that the journal was important, but he didn't want to let it out of his sight until Nik had a chance to read it.

"Shit," O'Donnell swore softly. "All right. I've trusted your gut so far in this case. I'll have to warn the mayor and commissioner about what's going on, but keep digging. If Vanderlist's our guy, you'll take him down, but I want it to be an iron-clad case."

"Thank you, Lieutenant."

"I'm going to have one of the uniforms drive your car back to the precinct. You take a cab back to your place." She strolled off.

Bobby grabbed his jacket and briefcase before gesturing to Nik. "Let's get out of here before she wonders why you're standing like that."

"Like what?" Nik glanced down at his stomach.

"Like you're hiding something under your shirt." He walked them past the barricade to the corner where he flagged down a cab.

"Why didn't you tell her about the journal? I'm pretty sure this would be considered withholding evidence and is probably illegal." Nik slipped into the back seat of the cab.

"We'll discuss it when we get to my house."

He wasn't about to talk about the case in the back of a taxicab. God knew if the driver listened in, he could sell the information to a newspaper or TV station and Bobby wasn't going to let his case get tossed out because of leaks to the media.

"Okay."

He wrapped his arm around Nik's shoulder and pulled the smaller man closer to him, burying his face in Nik's curls. Taking a deep breath, he inhaled the scent of smoke and cursed silently to himself.

So close. Twice he'd been so close to losing the man in his arms and all because he'd drawn him into the case. Of course, if it wasn't for the case, he would never have met Professor Nikolay Radin. They definitely didn't run in the same crowds. He smiled. Nik didn't emerge from his house or the library long enough to meet anybody.

"We need to go to my house, so I can get some clothes and my school stuff." Nik snuggled closer. "I assume you're not going to let me stay by myself."

"Hell no. This is the second time someone's tried to hurt you. I'm not going to risk you again. Anyone who tries to harm you again, I'll do whatever I can to stop them."

Nik eased back a few inches to study him for a moment. Bobby didn't care what the cabbie thought. Leaning down, he pressed their lips together, sweeping his tongue in to stroke over Nik's. His lover shivered and moaned, gripping Bobby's shoulders as they kissed. He almost pulled Nik onto his lap when the cabbie coughed.

Nik jerked away and his cheeks turned beet red. "Sorry," Nik murmured to the cabbie.

"No big deal, but where am I taking y'all?"

"To Chelsea first."

"Okay."

After getting Nik's belongings, they headed to Bobby's apartment. Bobby sent Nik in to take a shower while he set up the camera to download. He didn't touch the journal after Nik warned him against even breathing on it. He opened his briefcase and pulled out the folder with all his case notes.

Bobby's phone rang as the water shut off in his bathroom. Wandering to his bedroom to grab a pair of sweats and a T-shirt, he checked the ID display.

"Hey, Jablonsky. What's up?"

"You can tell me all about Thompson's place burning down when you meet me in the Village."

"And why am I going to the Village?" He tensed, reaching for pants and a dress shirt instead.

"We have another body in an alley behind *The Copa*."

Bobby heard everything Jablonsky didn't say.

"Fuck me." He slammed the closet door shut and perched on the edge of his bed.

"Yeah, partner. I think you need to get down here."

Nik walked into the bedroom and stopped when he saw Bobby on the phone.

"I'll leave here in ten. Be there as soon as I can."

"See you there."

He hung up and tossed the phone on the bed before changing his clothes. After going into the bathroom, he washed his face and hands. Nik was sitting on the bed when he returned to grab a tie.

"There's been another murder, hasn't there?"

Nik's low voice stopped him and he slumped next to his lover.

"Yes. The second in such a short time doesn't look good. I just hope we catch a lucky break soon, or there could be more deaths before this is over."

"You and Detective Jablonsky are good at your job, I'm sure, or your boss would never have put you on the case. I know you'll catch the person doing this, Bobby. I believe in you."

The touch of Nik's hand rubbing over his shoulder eased some of Bobby's tension. "All three of us will figure this out. We wouldn't be anywhere near as far on this case without you."

He stood with a sigh. "We brought that black light of yours. Why don't you look at the journal while I'm gone? Remember, don't open the door to anyone. You should be safe here."

Leaning over, Bobby gave Nik a quick kiss. He grabbed his gun and other stuff off the hallway table and headed out to his car. In no time at all, he was in the Village. He recognised the name of the club as being a pretty popular gay hang-out. He'd even gone there when he was younger and enjoyed looking for a warm body to share some time with.

The yellow crime scene tape was already up when he got there. Jablonsky waved at him from the entrance of the alley. Ducking under the tape, he joined his partner who led him to where a body lay, covered with a sheet.

Bobby crouched and tugged the sheet back. The first thing he noticed was the jagged wound in the young man's neck with what looked like teeth marks around the edges.

"Definitely has all the marks of our killer," he said softly.

"That's what I thought, and we know that little detail hasn't been leaked yet." Jablonsky drummed his pen against his leg.

Time to look at the victim's face. Bobby hated that part most of all. Studying the lifeless eyes and slack mouth depressed him, knowing that at one time, this boy really had been happy and full of life. Now he was dead in an alley, drained of blood and out of time.

"Holy fuck."

"What?"

"I saw this kid earlier when I went to Thompson's house. He was standing at the gate, told me he knew Thompson, and doubted the man did what the papers said he did."

"No shit?" Jablonsky shook his head. "Here's another thing for you. Mavis Vanderlist was last seen leaving *The Copa* on the night she was murdered."

Chapter Eleven

After shutting his apartment door, Bobby leaned against it for a moment with a sigh. God, at times, his job really sucked.

"Bobby?" Nik called.

"Yeah."

He toed off his shoes and shoved them to the side. He hung up his jacket and, as he loosened his tie, made his way into the living room where he found Nik curled up in his chair, the book they'd saved open on his lap.

Bobby strolled over, carefully put the book on the coffee table and swept Nik up into his arms. He embraced the slender man as he sat, settling Nik on his lap, burying his face in Nik's dark curls. Nik's familiar scent eased Bobby, almost like coming home did.

"I hate my job sometimes," he muttered.

Nik rubbed his shoulders the best he could while keeping the book from falling off. "Was it bad?"

"Not as bloody as the others, but he was just a kid." He drew a shuddering breath. "In fact, it was the same kid we saw outside Thompson's house before it burned."

He caught Nik as the man jerked upright.

"You're joking?"

Bobby rested his head on the back of the chair while watching Nik. "No, I'm not. You want another coincidence?"

When Nik nodded, Bobby pulled out some papers Jablonsky had handed him when they left the scene. Flipping through them, he found the right one and shuffled it to the top of the pile.

"Seems our other victim, Mavis Vanderlist, was last seen at *The Copa* where the body was found."

A frown marred Nik's smooth forehead. "You said found. Don't you think the kid was killed there?"

"No. First, I don't think the kid was old enough to get into the club." He waited until that sank in before continuing. "Second, there wasn't any blood. The victim bled out somewhere else and got dumped in the alley."

"If there's no blood, why do you think it's connected with the other killings?" Nik picked at his thumb.

Bobby grabbed Nik's hands and held them, not wanting him to do any more damage to his poor thumb. "There were bite marks on the neck where the wound sliced through the jugular. It wasn't nearly as messy as Thompson's killings or even Vanderlist's murder."

"And that means what?"

"It means whoever killed Vanderlist murdered this kid. It's all tied to that fucking wine and that sickening Knights society. I'm afraid what it also means is that the killer was not as overwhelmed by the blood lust like Thompson was. So he either knows what the wine is or does, or he isn't drinking it nearly as fast as Thompson did."

After climbing to his feet, Nik paced, his white knuckled grip on the book in his hands a sign of his agitation. Bobby tracked his lover's movements from one end of the living room to the other.

"What's wrong?"

Nik waved a hand at the journal in his hand. "I need to tell you what I found."

Before Nik could continue, Bobby's phone rang.

"Shit." He flipped it open and answered. "There better not be another murder."

"If there is, no one's reported it yet." Jablonsky laughed harshly. "I wanted to give you a heads up, buddy."

"Why?" He stood, and headed towards his bedroom. "I haven't done anything wrong."

"Ummm… I'm not sure, but having a crime scene burn down while you're searching it might be considered wrong."

"I didn't start the damn fire. Whoever it was knew what we were going to find at Thompson's house, Jablonsky, and I bet it was whoever killed that boy."

He unbuttoned his shirt and shrugged it off, tossing it in the direction of his laundry basket. Off came his belt, then his pants, until he stood in his room wearing only his underwear.

"I don't think the lieutenant can chew my ass too hard for that. Besides, we found something that might help us figure this whole mess out." He hesitated.

His inner voice questioned whether he should tell Jablonsky about the journal, or wait until he heard what Nik had to say.

"Seriously?"

"Yeah, I think so." Bobby opened his closet and yanked out a pair of jeans.

"You think so? This case is fucking dynamite, Bobby. You better have more than you think so or else we're going to explode. I don't want to pick up the pieces of my career because you think so." Jablonsky didn't sound happy.

"Hey, I just found the evidence. I haven't gotten a chance to go over it. Nik has though, and before you called me, he was going to tell me what he found in it. I should be able to tell you more tomorrow."

Pulling on his jeans, he zipped them, but left them unbuttoned. He didn't bother with a T-shirt. His apartment was warm enough. Scratching his chest, he wandered back out to the living room where Nik perched on the edge of the couch, tension in every line of his body.

"Fuck. Here comes the lieutenant and she doesn't look happy. I'll see you tomorrow when you'll bring me up-to-date with what you've got." Jablonsky hung up.

Bobby shut his phone and flopped onto the cushions beside Nik. He ran his hand down Nik's spine, bringing it to a stop at the small of his lover's back. Nik quivered and held out one of the reports Bobby had dropped when he went to change his clothes.

"Did you read this?"

Bobby took the paper and shook his head. "No. Jablonsky gave them to me right before I left the scene. Haven't had time to read anything more than the report on Vanderlist's last known whereabouts. What about it?"

"Just read it."

"I will in a second." Bobby set it on the coffee table before sliding his hand around the back of Nik's head and bringing the man to him. "I want to kiss you hello."

"Oh." Nik breathed, his green eyes wide behind his glasses.

The first touch of Nik's soft lips against his mouth brought a sigh from Bobby. Nik tasted perfect, like all of

Bobby's dreams come true. His anger and sadness at the young man's death faded until all he could think of was the way Nik melted into his arms.

He wrapped his other arm around Nik's waist, urging him to rest against his chest. Nik buried his hands in Bobby's hair, and tilted his head, letting the kiss go deeper. Their tongues teased and stroked. They sucked and nibbled.

It was the best welcome home Bobby had gotten in a long time and he decided he didn't want to go back to not having anyone waiting for him. Yet he understood it wasn't the right moment to tell Nik that. The middle of a gruesome murder investigation wasn't the best place to confess he was falling in love.

Nik straddled his lap, rocking their groins together. Bobby's moan got swallowed by Nik. It was going to get hot and heavy soon, but Bobby didn't mind. There would be enough time to discuss the case later.

The phone began to ring.

"Fuck." Bobby swore softly and rested his forehead against Nik's for a moment while he caught his breath.

"Your friends have bad timing," Nik commented before climbing off him.

"Tell me about it." He grabbed the phone and snarled as he brought it up to his ear. "This had better be a fucking emergency."

"When I'm done telling you, you might consider it one, Marks." His lieutenant's voice shot over the phone like a bullet.

"Sorry, Lieutenant." He climbed to his feet and went to rest his ass on the dining room table, knowing if he didn't get away from Nik, he wouldn't be able to keep from touching him. It wasn't good to grope your boyfriend while on the phone with your boss.

"Well, to tell you the truth, I feel like biting someone's head off at the moment, so I know how you feel." Her anger burned hot in her voice.

"What's up?"

"I just got off the phone with the commissioner. The man is a pain in the ass and an arrogant bastard. No wonder he and the mayor get along so well."

Something told Bobby he wasn't going to like what the lieutenant had to tell him.

"And you talked about me?"

She snorted. "He yelled about you, and I tried to reason with him, but he's got a hard-on for you, Marks, ever since the last Policeman's Ball where you punched his kid."

"How was I supposed to know that was his kid? All I saw was some guy kissing a girl who wasn't happy about it. I intervened and the guy swung at me. I'm not going to let anyone hit me." He frowned, remembering how angry the commissioner was to find his son unconscious and Bobby standing over him.

"I don't care what the reason was. The commissioner wants you off this case. He says the fact you let the Thompson house burn down was a clear sign that you're incompetent. Oh, and the gall you have of even daring to investigate Mr. Vanderlist is monumental. Vanderlist is an upstanding citizen who has lost his only child. Blah. Blah. Blah."

Bobby swung around and slammed his fist into the wall. "Are you fucking kidding me? I didn't allow the damn house to burn down. It was all I could do to save Nik and myself. And Vanderlist has a cigar box with the same seal that was on the wine bottle. How can he take me off the case?"

Nik studied him with a concerned expression, but stayed silent. Rage swelled in Bobby. He hit the wall again. *Fuck.* He might have pushed the boundaries in the pursuit of investigations, but never crossed any lines of propriety.

"He's the commissioner. He can take anyone off any case he wants. Unfortunately, you must have upset Vanderlist and he talked to the commissioner. Vanderlist is a huge donor and you know, the commissioner is thinking about running for the senate next year. He's not going to run the risk of pissing the man off and losing his support." The lieutenant growled under her breath. "I'm sorry, but I have to take you off this case."

"Okay. I understand, Lieutenant. It makes me mad as hell, but I know you can't do anything about it." A thought hit him. "I think I should take some of my vacation time."

"Now?" Suspicion coloured her voice.

"Why not? This case was the only one I was working at the moment. It's time I relaxed a little." He grinned at Nik. "Especially since I have something to fill my hours now."

Nik ducked his head and blushed, drawing a silent chuckle from Bobby.

"Fill out the papers and have them on my desk tomorrow morning. I'll approve it. That way you'll get paid." A pause. "Don't think I don't know what you're doing, Marks."

"Just taking some vacation time before I lose it. You're always on Jablonsky and me to take it."

"Right. Just keep in touch with Jablonsky."

He set the phone on the counter after the lieutenant hung up. Nik came up to him and wrapped his arms around his waist.

"I'm sorry."

Bobby frowned. "About what?"

"Getting taken off the case." Nik snuggled close, offering him comfort.

Nuzzling Nik's cheek, Bobby hummed in pleasure at the feel of Nik's slender body tight to his. "I'm not on the case anymore, at least officially. Even though I'm taking a vacation, my lieutenant knows I'll keep working on it. Especially now that the kid was murdered."

Nik stepped back and grabbed Bobby's hand. "Good to know, because you need to read the results of the tests on the wine."

"Why?" He let Nik drag him back to the couch where the papers were scattered over the cushions along with the journal Nik had been reading.

"Because if I'm reading the results right, then it coincides with what's in the journal. It could explain why the wine affects the drinker the way it does."

"Am I going to need a beer?"

Nik grinned. "You got any whisky?"

Bobby whistled. "That bad, huh?"

Nik rarely drank, but even he knew he could use something. "Make it two."

Bobby disappeared into the kitchen and came back with two highball glasses. He handed one to Nik and made himself comfortable in the corner of the couch.

As much as Nik wanted to crawl back into his lover's lap, he stopped himself. *Business first.* "I think it might be better to start with the journal."

Bobby nodded and took another sip of his drink.

Nik carefully picked up the journal he'd saved from the fire. "This was written by the grandson of Radu Cel Frumos' servant and lover, Dumitru Blaga. The grandson, Mihail Cuza wrote the stories his grandfather told him. Dumitru was only fifteen when he was deemed too old to take to bed in Radu's eyes, so although I've no doubt most of what I read is true, keep an open mind that Dumitru was a scorned lover."

Bobby nodded and sat up a little straighter. "Go on."

"There's a lot of the history of the time period, but if you don't mind, I'm going to break it down and give you the *Reader's Digest* version."

Bobby chuckled. "I'd appreciate that."

"Okay. According to the journal, Radu and Vlad III, the man everyone knows as Vlad the Impaler, hated each other, which actually was pretty common for the time period. Brothers fought brothers and fathers for seats in power. Anyway, Vlad III wanted his father's throne, but his brother Mircea II was next in line. In a bold move, Vlad III ordered his private army to track down his father and brother and have them killed."

Nik glanced up from the journal. "Here's where it gets interesting. Radu found out about the plot and sent his own men to try and warn his father and brother. He also sent his servant, Dumitru with special instructions in case his men were too late to stop the deaths. As it happens, they *were* too late. Dumitru followed his instructions and dug the bodies up from their hastily buried graves, and drained the blood from both victims."

He noticed Bobby stiffen.

"Do you want me to go on?" he asked.

"Yes."

"Dumitru gave Radu the vessels containing his own father and brother's blood. Radu instructed a local winemaker to mix the container's contents with a batch of specially prepared wine."

Bobby's face screwed up in disgust, Nik couldn't blame him. The details of what Radu did were disgusting.

"According to Dumitru, the winemaker gave him six specially designed casks of the tainted wine which he took back to Radu. Then there's a strange entry about Dumitru spying on Radu as his master performed 'The Ritual', whatever that is. It goes on to talk about Radu slicing open his own chest, smearing his body with the blood and chanting in a language Dumitru didn't understand."

"Devil worship?" Bobby questioned.

Nik shook his head. "Sounds like it to me. Whatever it was, Radu didn't seem to suffer much. According to Dumitru, hours later, he appeared stronger than ever. Dumitru was given orders to send one cask to Vlad III on the eve of his celebratory dinner for gaining the seat of power. Vlad III, drank the wine his brother, Radu had sent and that was the beginning of Vlad III's blood lust."

"He began drinking people's blood?" Bobby asked.

Nik nodded his head. "That's an understatement. He not only consumed the blood of his servants and ladies of the court, but began openly fucking his soldiers and feeding from them as well. People seemed drawn to Vlad like never before. The more insane he became, the more people offered themselves to him. The carnage of his battles was legendary, but after a while, he began to slow down. His desire for blood waned, and his people began to lose interest in following him. That's how Radu was able to take the power away from him."

Nik picked up his glass and took a drink. He noticed Bobby's glass was completely empty. Without being asked, he rose and retrieved the bottle of whisky from the kitchen. He handed it to Bobby.

"Thanks."

He bent and gave his lover a quick kiss before continuing. "By then, Dumitru had been replaced in Radu's bed by a younger servant. He was extremely bitter and went to Vlad III and told him what his brother had done. Vlad asked Dumitru if there was any of the wine left, and Dumitru told him there were two casks, knowing there were actually five. He figured he could use the other three casks at a later time to bargain for either Vlad or Radu's favours."

Nik paused. He knew this was all new to Bobby. Because Nik felt at ease in front of a classroom, giving lectures, he needed to make sure Bobby was keeping up with him.

"You okay?" he asked as Bobby poured more whisky into his glass.

Bobby nodded. "Keep going."

Nik nodded. "After consuming two more casks of the tainted wine, Vlad once again became the charismatic man he'd enjoyed being earlier, but to a higher degree. He regained his seat of power and waged an all out war. This was the period in which he became known as Vlad the Impaler, later to be immortalised by Bram Stoker's Dracula. According to Dumitru, rumours began to circulate that Vlad was consuming large amounts of blood trying to maintain the edge the casks of wine had given him. Some theorized it was Vlad's way of *feeding the demon within him*. Dumitru knew he wasn't safe, that in his insanity, Vlad would go after him. He fled with the three remaining casks to Greece, where he married, sired a son and made his son vow to protect the casks at all costs."

"And somehow those casks ended up five hundred years later at an auction in New York?" Bobby questioned.

Nik carefully opened the journal and extracted an engraved invitation and passed it to Bobby. "I found this."

Bobby took the card. "I need to call Jablonsky."

"There's more. The lab report you received indicates two sources of DNA in the wine. It was the real stuff. I wonder…if the wine was able to make a man insane five hundred and sixty-three years ago, what are its capabilities after maturing for that many years?"

While Bobby called his partner, Nik carefully wrapped the journal in its cloth and put it in the new messenger bag he'd purchased. He hoped Bobby wouldn't turn it over to Jablonsky, but he knew his lover would do what he thought was best for the investigation.

With the business side of the evening over, Nik curled up on the couch next to Bobby and waited patiently for him to finish his call. His mind kept returning to the passage about the demon being inside Vlad and the demon's need for blood to keep it alive. He'd never believed in the supernatural, but it made as much sense as blood tainted wine driving businessmen to rip out the throats of innocent people.

"Okay, keep me in the loop as much as you can," Bobby told his partner before hanging up.

As soon as Bobby was finished, Nik took the invitation out of his hand. "Did you notice this?"

Bobby stared at the raised seal at the top of the cardstock. "Yeah. I didn't tell Jablonsky about it though. Do you think The Knights of Paiderastia were the only ones to receive these?"

"I do. If Jablonsky can track down the auctioneer and get a list of who the invitations went out to, we'll have a list of the society's members."

Bobby pulled Nik in for a deep kiss. Nik melted against his lover's chest as his mouth was thoroughly fucked.

"Ready for bed?" Nik asked, coming up for air.

"Beyond ready." Bobby tried to stand with Nik still wrapped around him and nearly toppled them both over the coffee table. "Shit."

Nik laughed and got his feet under him. "Might be safer if I just walked with you to the bedroom."

"But not nearly as much fun." Bobby reached down and gave Nik's ass a squeeze.

Nik enjoyed this playful side to his lover. He took several steps before he began to undress. With his shirt tossed to the floor, he walked backward while he pushed down his oversized sweats.

Bobby groaned and reached for Nik's cock.

Laughing, Nik shook his finger. "Uh. Uh. Uh. You're next."

While Bobby struggled to push his jeans down and off, Nik rounded the corner leading to the bedroom. He launched himself onto the mattress, and with a quick change in positions, he was on his knees with his ass facing the door by the time Bobby came into the room.

"Well, isn't that a pretty sight."

Nik spread his knees even more, opening himself fully to his lover's gaze. "It's all yours. Come and get it."

One moment he was teasing Bobby, and the next a wet tongue ran up the length of his crack before moving back down to rim the puckered skin. "Oh, fuck."

Bobby chuckled and continued to lap and drill at Nik's hole.

The scrape of teeth against his sensitive skin sent Nik's back bowing towards the mattress. *Oh God.* He reached under him and wrapped his hand around his cock, applying a firm grip. "I'm gonna come."

Bobby removed his face from the crack of Nik's ass and grabbed a condom and the lubricant from the bedside table. He entered Nik's hole with a lubed finger and began to saw in and out. "Hard and fast, or soft and sweet?"

Nik tightened his grip on his cock. "Just fuck me."

Bobby chuckled again and removed his finger. Nik heard the crinkling sound of the foil as Bobby opened and rolled on the condom. After several cool drops of lube dripped down the crevice of his ass, Nik felt the blunt head of Bobby's cock as it slowly pushed inside.

He blew out several calming breaths as the pain threatened to overwhelm him. Bobby's cock was bigger than an average man, and Nik hadn't given his lover proper time to stretch him.

Once Bobby's cock was fully seated, Nik waited for that moment when pain turned to pleasure. He was grateful he didn't have to wait long. "Okay."

His hands gripping Nik's hips, Bobby began a slow rhythm in and out. "Let me know how you're feeling."

Nik's brain was so muddled with pleasure, he wasn't sure he understood the question. "How I'm feeling? Well, I think I'm falling in love with you."

Bobby paused mid-stroke. "Although that wasn't what I meant by the question, it's good to know."

Embarrassed, Nik buried his head in the blankets.

He received a nip on the shoulder and a nuzzle to the neck. "I feel the same way. In case you were wondering."

Nik grinned. He knew how easy it was to say things you didn't mean in the heat of sex, but he really wanted to believe Bobby's words.

His declaration must've done something to Bobby, because his lover picked up, not only his speed, but the intensity of his thrusts. At that moment, Nik didn't care. He was lost in sensations beyond his wildest dreams. Never had he been with a lover with such passion.

Had the bedspread been any rougher, Nik knew he'd have come away from their session with a burn on his cheek. As it was, the flesh was becoming sensitive as it rubbed against the material underneath.

With his free hand, Nik reached back towards Bobby, needing something of his lover to hang onto.

Bobby's thrusts slowed. "Is something wrong?"

Nik tried to calm his beating heart enough to speak. "No. Need to touch you."

Bobby pulled out and flipped Nik to his back. He positioned Nik's legs over his shoulders and entered him once again. "Touch me."

Nik smiled into his lover's eyes and ran his hands over Bobby's lightly furred chest. "You are so fucking unbelievable."

After several deep thrusts, Bobby removed Nik's legs and lay on top of him. He rubbed his lips against Nik's for several passes before settling on them. The kiss was gentle even as Bobby's cock continued to ravage Nik's hole.

Nik slid his tongue against Bobby's, playing charge and retreat as the pleasure continued to build. "I need…"

Bobby repositioned enough to rub against Nik's cock.

"Yes!" Nik howled, arching his back as he warmed the area between their bodies with his seed.

Bobby reached above Nik's head and grabbed the edge of the mattress as he hammered his cock in and out of Nik's hole.

"Feels. So. Good!" Bobby punctuated with each thrust before burying his cock deep.

Nik held onto his lover as Bobby stiffened and came, the aftershocks causing Bobby to jerk and buck against him. Nik threaded his fingers through the short, sweaty hair on the back of Bobby's head and pulled him into another kiss. With every flick of his tongue, he mentally cried his love for the man in his arms. Never would there be another lover that could compare to his detective.

Chapter Twelve

A buzzing sound woke Bobby up the next day.

What the hell?

Bobby blinked, staring up at his bedroom ceiling as he worked out what the noise filling the air was.

"Are you going to shut that off?"

Turning his head to the left, he met Nik's dark green eyes. A frown marred his lover's forehead. Bobby realised the alarm on his clock was the culprit. He flung his hand out, knocking the offending thing to the floor.

"Who set the alarm?" He certainly didn't remember doing it.

"I did." Nik sat up and stretched, displaying a lot of pale skin to Bobby's devouring gaze.

"Why?" He muttered, not really listening for an answer.

Bobby trailed his fingers over Nik's stomach and down the thin line of hair leading under the blankets. Nik shifted closer, allowing Bobby to slip his hand in between his legs to cup his balls. He squeezed gently, and Nik moaned.

"I have classes today." Nik spread his thighs and rocked into Bobby's hand.

"Really?" He slid his fingers further down to rub over Nik's hole while he sucked on Nik's nipple.

"Umm...yes?"

He chuckled and pressed his finger inside Nik. "You don't sound sure."

Rocking, Nik groaned as he took a second finger. Bobby wrapped his other hand around Nik's cock and pumped in time with Nik's rhythm. God, he loved the sounds Nik made when he was coming. A twist of his hand over the top of Nik's shaft gathered some pre-cum and eased the friction a little.

"Come on, baby," he urged.

"Bobby!"

Nik climaxed and wet heat spilled over Bobby's hand. He slowly eased off the strokes until Nik slumped back against the pillows and his cock softened.

"Good morning." He brushed a kiss over Nik's mouth before climbing out of bed to head towards the bathroom.

"What about you?" Nik gestured at Bobby's erection.

"I'll be all right. I can wait until we have enough time to take it slow. You need to get ready for the day."

He cleaned up in the bathroom and headed back to pull on some jeans and a T-shirt. Nik took a shower while Bobby made breakfast. His lover joined him at the table.

"Do you have everything you need for your classes, or do we need to stop by your house?" He scooped some eggs onto his toast and took a bite.

"No. I have what I need. I'll be taking the journal with me, so I can study it more." Nik shifted. "What are you doing today while I'm teaching students?"

After taking a sip of his orange juice, he grinned. "I plan on turning in my vacation forms then I'll take Jablonsky out to lunch. I want to know if he's found anything out about the auction and auctioneer. That's after I drop you off at the university, because I'm not letting you take that journal on the bus. I shouldn't even be letting you take it anywhere. I should have turned it in to Jablonsky the moment I knew you had it."

Nik shook his head. "I need to study it more. The answers are in that journal, Bobby, and I just need to dig a little deeper. You can give it to your partner when I'm done, and you don't have to escort me, Bobby. I can take the bus."

"No. I told you before, I don't like you taking public transportation." He cleaned his plate and stood, taking it to the sink where he rinsed it before putting it in the dishwasher. "Okay. I'll let you 'borrow' it for another day, but after that, I'm turning it over to Jablonsky. One more day, Nik, and until I turn it in, I'm making sure you and it are safe."

"I think you're a snob and spoiled from driving that car of yours around," Nik teased.

They cleaned up the kitchen, moving around each other like they'd been together for years. Bobby put on his boots and grabbed his keys as he waited by the door for Nik.

"Ready?"

"Yeah." Nik rewrapped the journal and carefully placed it in his backpack before leading the way out.

Bobby stared at Nik's firm ass covered in khaki fabric as they went downstairs to the parking lot. They got in the car and headed towards the university.

"Call me when you're done for the day, and I'll come pick you up." He stopped in front of the history building.

Nik rolled his eyes, but didn't say anything as he started to leave the car. Bobby reached out and grabbed Nik's arm, tugging him back for a kiss.

"I love you," he murmured against Nik's lips.

"Love you too." Nik blushed and exited the Camaro in a hurry.

Bobby waited until Nik entered the building before he drove away.

Forty minutes later, he stepped off the elevator onto the Homicide floor. He nodded to several of his fellow detectives while heading to his desk. The appropriate forms rested in the middle of his blotter. Jablonsky wasn't around, so Bobby started filling out the papers for his vacation.

By the time he finished all of the forms, Jablonsky was back.

"You hand in those papers yet?"

"No. Just signing my name to them. I'll drop them off to the lieutenant in a minute." He glanced around. "Can I buy you some coffee? Maybe an early lunch?"

"Sounds good to me. I'll meet you downstairs at your car." Jablonsky strolled from the room without looking back.

Bobby gathered his forms and went to the lieutenant's office, knocking on the door.

"Come in," she called.

"Here's my vacation requests, Lieutenant." He set them on her desk.

She nodded. "I'll sign them and make sure they get filed right away. As of right now, you're on paid vacation for how many weeks?" She shot him a look.

"Ah…I think I have three weeks coming to me."

"Three weeks is fine. Of course, if something comes up before that, then we'll see."

"Yes, ma'am." Bobby smiled slightly and left her office.

Jablonsky was standing next to Bobby's car when he got downstairs. His partner knew better than to lean against the Camaro. Bobby waved his hand towards the car.

"Get in. We'll go to that deli you like so much, and you can tell me what you know."

"Are you lodging a complaint about being taken off the case?" Jablonsky shook his head.

"No. I'm using my vacation time. The lieutenant didn't have a problem with it." Driving to the deli, he parked.

They waited until they were seated and had their coffee before continuing the conversation.

"Did you tell the lieutenant where you got the information about the auction house?"

Jablonsky shook his head. "No. I told her I figured it out through the process of elimination. I went to talk to the auctioneer. Guess what I found him doing when I got there."

"I can't begin to guess."

"He was burning some papers." Jablonsky shook his head. "Not sure what else he managed to burn, but I rescued this from him. I made a copy for you since I had to log it in as evidence."

"Good man."

He took the copy from Jablonsky and scanned it quickly. "Fuck, did you see the names on this list?"

"Yeah. Unfortunately, it was on fire when I got there, so the bottom half of the sheet is gone. Which is irritating because what if the person we're looking for was on the list?"

Bobby checked the names again. "Thompson's name is on here, along with Vanderlist. Do you think the men on this list are members of that society?"

"Makes sense. When I pressed the auctioneer, he said that the person who put the casks up for sale set it up as a private invitation only auction. He was sent that list of potential buyers. No one else could bid or was allowed into the auction."

Sipping his coffee, Bobby thought for a few minutes. He sighed and looked at Jablonsky.

"Guess I know what I'll be doing during my vacation."

His partner grinned. "I don't envy you."

"I really didn't want to spend my free time trailing Vanderlist around." He folded the list and tucked it in his pocket. "Did you get me the licence numbers for his vehicles and the addresses of places I could find him?"

"Yeah. Here you go. I'd have emailed them to you, but I know how much you hate checking your email." Jablonsky smirked at him.

He flipped the man off before grabbing the paper and going over the addresses. "I'll have to go to my place and get my camera."

"Do you really think Vanderlist would have killed his own daughter?" Jablonsky kept his voice low.

Bobby shrugged. "We've seen it before. Even rich guys kill their families. He has some big secrets to hide. What if his daughter found out he was a member of that society?"

"I guess that would be a reason to kill her. It would ruin him if it got out that he liked boys." Jablonsky stared down into his cup. "Did you see some of those names, Bobby? Some pretty well known men are on there. What would happen if that list got leaked?"

"It better not get leaked. We can't risk Vanderlist running. If he is the murderer, I need to get proof for you before more people die. Especially in such a gory manner."

"The wine is causing it?" Jablonsky didn't sound like he believed it.

"That's what Nik thinks. The test shows that there is human DNA in the wine, so someone's blood got mixed in with it. I still don't understand how it worked, but everything we've learned says that it drove someone mad when it was first bottled. I don't doubt it could cause someone to kill now."

Bobby pushed to his feet, throwing money on the table to cover their coffee. He and Jablonsky shoved their way through the growing crowd until they were outside.

"I'll grab a cab back to the precinct. You might want to start following Vanderlist around this afternoon. See if he does anything suspicious during the day."

"Thanks. I'll call you later, if I get anything you should know."

They shook hands and Jablonsky headed off to flag down a cab. Bobby jumped in his car, planning his course of action. Stopping by his apartment for his camera was first on his list, before tracking Vanderlist down and dogging his every step until the case broke.

Trailing Vanderlist would cut into his time with Nik, but he hoped his lover would understand.

* * * *

Bobby's phone rang and as he picked it up, he glanced at his watch. It had to be Nik.

"Hello?"

"Hey."

Nik's voice caused Bobby's heart to skip a beat and he rolled his eyes at himself. When had he turned into a sap?

"How'd your classes go, Professor Radin?" He set his camera down on the passenger seat and started his car.

"Good. Some kids really listened. Others are there for the credits, not for the knowledge."

"Sounds like it's been a normal day."

Checking behind him, he pulled into traffic. He'd pick up Nik, and grab dinner before taking him home. He had to get back to Vanderlist's house before the man decided to go out for the night.

Nik chuckled. "You're right. It was a normal day. How was yours?"

"I need to talk to you about that." He stopped at a light and frowned. "I won't be able to stay in with you tonight. I have to tail Vanderlist to see if I can get anything on him."

"Okay." Disappointment coloured Nik's words.

"Jablonsky got a list from the auction place that was on the invitation. Vanderlist and Thompson were on it. I think it might be a list of society members. The auctioneer was burning it when Jablonsky got there."

The sharp inhale of breath told Bobby that Nik recognised the significance of the list. "The killer could be listed."

"Yeah. Unfortunately the bottom part of the paper was burnt, so we're missing half the names." Bobby switched lanes. "Sorry about tonight. Just one of the perks of dating a cop."

"I understand. I might not like it, but I can deal with it as long as you come back and sleep with me when you're done."

He smiled. "I think I can do that."

"Good. This killer needs to be caught, and if that means we don't get to spend every waking minute together, I'll sacrifice until you take him down."

"I knew there was a reason why I fell in love with you."

It was getting easier to say. He glanced at the street sign as he passed it.

"Hey, I'm about twenty minutes away. I'll pick you up and we can grab dinner before I get back to my post."

"I love you too. I'll be waiting outside. See you soon."

Nik hung up and Bobby set his phone in the console between the seats. He would make sure to take his time at dinner. No point rushing through it. He wanted to spend as much time with Nik as he could. It was a sure sign he was in love.

* * * *

Nik licked the barbeque sauce from his fingers, eyeing the mound of rib bones. "I won't be able to eat anything else for a week."

"You keep licking those fingers like that, and I have a feeling you'll be eating something else before you leave this table."

Nik chuckled. Bobby loved having his cock sucked. It had become one of their favourite pastimes. They'd retire to the couch after dinner and pretend to watch television. Of course Nik's head was usually busy bobbing up and down in his lover's lap by the second commercial break. Nik couldn't remember the last time he'd actually watched a full programme from beginning to end.

Finished with dinner, Nik stood and straddled Bobby's lap. "You needing?"

"Wanting is more like it. The blow job you gave me in the car earlier was only the second one that Camaro has ever played a part in."

Nik stuck his fingers in his ears. "La la la. I can't hear you."

Chuckling, Bobby reached out and pulled Nik's hands down. "I've had that car for a lot of years. Too many for you to get jealous over what I did or didn't do in it with an old lover."

Nik wiggled his ass as he rubbed his hands against Bobby's chest. "Sorry. Doesn't matter. I'd much rather pretend I'm your one and only."

Bobby put his hand to the back of Nik's neck and pulled him in for a kiss. "You are my one and only."

"Mmmm." Nik moaned as he kissed his lover again, sliding his tongue across Bobby's. "Are you sure you don't want company on your stakeout?"

Bobby squeezed Nik's ass. "How much surveying do you think the two of us would get done if we were shut up together in a car all night?"

Nik knew it wasn't practical, but he'd gotten used to his evenings with Bobby. "I guess I'll have to entertain myself then."

Bobby ran his finger down the seam of Nik's pants, pressing against his hole through the material. "Not too much playing. If you're still horny when I get home, I'll take care of you."

Nik snuggled against Bobby's chest. "You always do."

After giving Nik's ass one last squeeze, Bobby gave him a playful slap. "Let me up, you cock hungry beast. I've got work to do and killers to catch."

Nik stood and readjusted his erection. "The sacrifices I make for the safety of my fellow man."

Bobby led Nik to the door and gave him one last kiss before grabbing up his small duffle. "Make sure you lock up behind me."

"I will." Nik buried his face in Bobby's neck and inhaled. "I'll miss you."

Bobby grinned. "You're getting spoiled."

"Uh huh. Remember that when you're sitting in the car with no one to suck your cock."

* * * *

Nik was busy cleaning the kitchen when his cell phone rang. He dried his hands and ran into the living room, snatching the phone from off the coffee table. "Hello?"

"Hi, Nik," Professor George Lattimer greeted.

"Hi, Professor. I hope you have news for me." Nik hadn't told the professor about the journal, but he'd spoken to Bobby about it, and they both agreed if it became necessary to bring in the professor's expertise they would.

"Maybe. The label under the seal isn't going to be much help. It says 'Wine is sweet but vengeance is sweeter'."

Nik nodded. "That makes sense."

There was a pause on the other end of the phone. "What aren't you telling me?"

Shit. "I found a journal written by Radu cel Frumos' servant. It chronicles secret ceremonies the servant witnessed Radu and the other Knights of Paiderastia performing. Along with the making of six casks of wine and what they were used for."

"And?"

"And it's not good." "I want that journal."

Nik was surprised at the vehemence of the request. As a matter of fact, it didn't sound like a request at all, more like an order. "I can't do that. It's part of the investigation."

"You've turned it over to the police!" George shouted in anger.

"No." Something told Nik he shouldn't say more. "Look, Professor, I shouldn't even have told you about it. Bobby will probably kill me when he finds out I did."

"Bobby isn't my main concern at the moment. That journal belongs in a museum."

"Yes, sir, I realise that. Once the investigation is over, it'll be up to the police." Nik prayed the professor wouldn't go over his head. The police didn't even know he had the journal, and Nik knew withholding evidence could get him into a shit load of trouble.

He wondered if he should throw the professor off by mentioning the list of names Jablonsky had discovered. He was contemplating when George spoke again.

"You call me with anything you find, hear me? I've told you before. This case is taking you way out of your depth of understanding. It's not only dangerous, but completely unprofessional of you to act in the capacity you are for an investigation you're not an expert on."

Nik reared back and held the phone away from his ear. Why did he suddenly feel like he'd just received a spanking, and not the good kind? "I'll speak with you later, Professor."

Nik hung up the phone before he said something he'd come to regret. He wondered if the professor was merely jealous of Nik's discovery. What would it be like to work your entire life and not find something as important as the journal was to world history, a subject George Lattimer had devoted his life to?

Nik flopped down on the sofa and turned on the television. He wasn't sure what he watched, his mind was occupied elsewhere.

Finally, at eleven o'clock, he gave up and went to bed. He thought about calling Bobby, but they hadn't discussed phone procedures on a stakeout. With the luck he'd had lately, Nik would probably call at the wrong time and alert Vanderlist of Bobby's presence.

He undressed quickly and climbed between the sheets, wishing Bobby was there with him.

Several hours later, a noise woke him. At first Nik thought it was Bobby. He crept out of bed and towards the living room when the noise came again. *Fuck.* Definitely not Bobby. Whoever was breaking in was doing it from the small fire escape landing off the kitchen. He scrambled back to the bedroom, grabbing his phone as he went.

He eased the door shut and called Bobby.

"Hey, babe."

"Someone's breaking in" Nik whispered, his hands shaking so badly he could barely hold the phone.

"Can you get out?"

"No. I'm in the bedroom."

"Get in the closet and stay there. I'm on my way."

Nik threw the covers up so the bed didn't look slept in and retreated to the closet by way of the city lights shining through the blinds. He tried to make himself as small as possible. "I'm scared."

"I know you are, baby. Just hold the line open. No more talking, okay?"

Despite Bobby's orders, Nik couldn't help but tell him how he felt in case it was the last time. "I love you."

"I love you, too. Listen, I'm going to put you on speaker, so you know you're not alone. Don't say anything just be as quiet as humanly possible."

Nik almost said okay, but stopped himself.

"I've lived quite a few years in this city, surrounded by millions of people and never did I hope to meet someone like you. You're the best thing that's ever happened to me, and I'll be damned if I'll let a prowler take you away from me."

Nik wanted to tell Bobby the person breaking in was after something specific. It broke his heart, but there was only one person who could be responsible for the burglary. It suddenly dawned on Nik. If something happened to him, Bobby needed to know.

Cupping his hand over the phone, he whispered. "I think Professor Lattimer might be behind the break-in."

"Lattimer? You can tell me why he'd be breaking into my apartment when I get there. In other words, you, my love, have some explaining to do."

Nik heard a crash in the living room and a loud curse. Whoever it was didn't care if he was heard or not. "Did you hear that?"

"Yeah. I heard. I'm about four blocks away. Hide behind my clothes as much as possible."

Nik felt around in the dark and grasped the laundry basket. He dumped the dirty clothes and tried to bury himself under them. *Please let this work.* He'd fallen in love for the first time in his life and he wasn't...

All thoughts stopped as he heard the front door open. Had the intruder left?

His heartbeat sounded in his ears as he waited. When the closet door was thrown open, Nik held his breath, his eyes squeezed shut.

"Nik!"

The clothes strewn on top of him were whisked away as he was pulled into the warm embrace of his lover. Nik's hands clutched the back of Bobby's shirt as he held on to his heart.

Bobby buried his face against Nik's hair. "I'm so glad I got here in time."

"Is he gone?"

Bobby nodded. "The door was wide open when I got here."

"Then you just missed him. Maybe you should..."

"No." Bobby shook his head. "The second you made the call, all I cared about was getting home to you. At that point I wasn't a cop. I was the man who loves you more than anything in this world."

Nik tried to control his shaking body, but soon came to realise he wasn't the only one trembling. He continued to hold onto Bobby until both their breathing returned to normal.

Bobby leant back and stared into Nik's eyes. "You okay?"

Nik nodded. "I told Lattimer about the journal, and he got really nasty with me. He wanted it. I told him he'd have to talk to the police about it after the investigation was over. Something tells me he didn't want to wait that long."

Bobby cursed, closing his eyes momentarily. "I thought he was your friend."

"Yeah, so did I." He couldn't admit to Bobby how much it hurt. He'd shared information with his mentor that could've gotten him killed. But it was the death of his friendship that made him want to break down in tears.

"Did he get it?" Nik asked.

"Probably. The room's a mess."

"It was in my messenger bag."

"Then they got it. But, he can't steal the knowledge we've already gained from it."

"Yeah, but we can't prove anything without the journal."

"We couldn't have proven anything with it anyway. Even though you and I know it was the real deal, I doubt even Lattimer could have proved it. Besides, we took it from a crime scene without handing it over."

"I took it, not you. I would've told them that."

"And I wouldn't have let you take the fall alone." Bobby kissed Nik's temple and set him on the floor. "I'm going to see what kind of damage I've got. Why don't you get back into bed?"

Nik watched Bobby walk from the room. He slowly got to his feet and made his way over to the bed. He sank down on the mattress feeling worse about himself than he had in a long time.

He was still in the same position when Bobby came back into the room. His lover began to undress. With his jeans pushed down to his thighs, Bobby fell to the bed. He scooted over to wrap an arm around Nik. "It's okay, babe. He's gone."

Nik shook his head. "It's not that."

"Then what is it? I can tell something's bothering you."

Nik took a deep breath and turned to face Bobby. "It seems like you're always saving me, and I know someday you're going to get tired of it. Maybe I should take some karate classes or something."

"What?" Bobby pulled Nik back until they were lying side by side. "I save people for a living, complete strangers. What kind of man would I be if I didn't do everything in my power to save the man I love?"

Still naked, Nik snuggled against Bobby. "Well, thank you for being that man for me."

Chapter Thirteen

Frowning, Bobby pried his eyes open and stared up at the dark ceiling. His cell phone rang again. He realised this was the sound that had woken him. Nik murmured and snuggled closer.

"Hey, sweetheart, you have to move." He pushed Nik gently away from him before reaching for the phone on the nightstand.

"You're on vacation," Nik muttered.

He chuckled as he answered the call.

"God, you sound cheerful for it being three in the morning." Jablonsky grumbled in his ear.

"I'm on vacation, Jablonsky. Not having to get up at a forsaken hour of the night means I can stay up doing other things."

Jablonsky grunted. "I don't even want to think about what you mean by that."

"What do you want? I doubt you called to find out what I'm doing."

After climbing out of bed, he turned to pat Nik on the ass and to make sure his lover was covered by the blankets.

"They found two more bodies."

"Fuck."

The curse burst from his throat, causing Nik to roll over and stare at him.

Bobby repeated Jablonsky's message to Nik while digging in his dresser for a clean shirt and socks.

"That means he's escalating, doesn't it?" Nik sat up, blankets pooling around his waist.

"I think so. It depends on if they were killed at the same time, or just dumped in the same place."

He tugged on his jeans, socks, and boots. "Where am I headed, Jablonsky?"

"You have to make sure no one sees you. The commissioner will get pissed if he finds out you showed up at a scene. Especially one that might be connected to the other killings."

"I'm not a rookie, Jablonsky. I know how to make sure I'm not seen by anyone who might tell the commissioner." Bobby leant over and kissed Nik. "I'll call you when I'm on my way back."

He headed down the hallway, holding his T-shirt while he finished talking to Jablonsky. "Where am I going?"

"Harlem." Jablonsky gave him the address. "It's an alley behind a pay-by-the-hour motel."

"I'll be there in thirty or so."

After ending the call, he set his phone on the entryway table and yanked on his T-shirt. He checked his gun before slipping it in his back holster, making sure the hem of his shirt hung over the grip. He was going into a hard part of town, and he didn't want to give anyone the chance to grab his sidearm.

"Bobby."

He turned and spied Nik leaning in the doorway, a sheet wrapped around his hips. Nik bit his bottom lip, worry clear in his eyes. Strolling back, he cupped Nik's cheek and stroked his thumb over his lover's chin.

"Keep the door locked and your phone close by. I don't think anyone will come back since they have what they want after taking that stupid journal. If you get worried, call me and I'll come back." He kissed Nik hard.

Nik slipped his hand around the back of Bobby's head, holding him close for a minute before letting him go. "Take care of yourself and tell Jablonsky I said hi."

"I will."

He headed out, running down the stairs out to his car. As he drove to Harlem, he thought about what finding two bodies meant.

Shit. When had Vanderlist found time to kill them? Bobby had been following the man for the last two days and had never seen anything that indicated the man was doing anything illegal. Of course, some of those evening meetings were probably with the other men on the auctioneer's list, but Bobby hadn't had time to run the licence numbers yet.

The twirling lights of the police cars alerted Bobby to which alley he had to go to. Locking the car, he wandered over to where the uniformed cops stood. Hansen didn't say a word or even look at him, just lifted the crime tape to allow him to slip under. No one else glanced in his direction and the stray thought crossed his mind. Was this what it felt like to be shunned?

Jablonsky waved to him, but didn't approach. Bobby stayed on the edges of the crowd, not interfering with the crime techs and the other detectives combing the scene.

He didn't even have to get close to spot that there wasn't a lot of blood pooling under the bodies. Just like the last victim, these people must have been killed and their blood either drained or consumed elsewhere. Shifting around, he got a good look at the wounds on the neck. *Damn.* More bite marks. Rubbing his chin, he turned away and moved back to his car.

"Marks."

Bobby stopped and rested his hip on the door of his car. Jablonsky jogged towards him.

"It doesn't look good."

"Killed somewhere else?" He stared down at his boots.

"Looks like it. The M.E. places their deaths at around nine or ten hours ago." Jablonsky flipped through his notebook, checking the facts he'd gotten from the techs so far.

"Both of them? How could he have done that, Jablonsky? Where does he take them? These last three murders have been far more thought out and controlled. If he's drinking that wine, he's manipulating the effects. That thought scares me." Bobby rubbed his palms on his thighs.

"The M.E. says they were killed around the same time. You're right. It can only get worse if we don't catch the bastard soon. I talked to the auctioneer again and he said there were three casks sold."

"Where did they go and who bought them?"

Jablonsky shrugged. "He didn't know. They were bought by shell companies. It'll take us a while to trace the different companies and who owns them."

His partner shot a look over his shoulder at the two body bags in the alley. "I don't think we have the time it's going to take. More kids are going to die."

"Kids?" Bobby pressed a fist to his stomach, hoping the nausea wouldn't overwhelm him and make him throw up like a rookie.

"Yep. Same as the last one." Jablonsky shook his head. "How's Nik doing?"

"He's still feeling a little violated and I'm sure it'll take a while for him to feel completely secure. But he knows that we have to catch the monster that's doing this to these kids. Nik's been very helpful with the whole thing." He scraped his boot heel on the sidewalk.

"Poor guy probably never expected to get caught up in something like this when you called to ask for his expertise."

Bobby chuckled. "You're right, but I think he needed his nice life shook up slightly."

"Shit. There's the lieutenant. You better head out. I'll email you the files on the case as soon as I get them from the coroner."

"Thanks."

He shook his partner's hand, nodded to his lieutenant, but climbed in the car before she could collar him. Digging through his stuff, he pulled out his log book to jot down his thoughts and what Jablonsky told him. He hated not being on the inside of the investigation. It drove him crazy because he figured he'd miss something or not be told the most inconsequential piece of information and that would be the piece that would break the whole thing wide open.

After starting the car, he eased into traffic to head back to his apartment. Two more young men dead. It had to be deeply connected to the society. Even though he'd worked more years than he wanted to think about on homicide and had seen some truly horrifying things, the thought of a society that condoned something like paedophilia made his skin crawl and his stomach churn. No one, boy or girl, should have their innocence taken from them like that.

His phone rang and he checked the number. Jablonsky. Was his partner calling him because the lieutenant chewed him out for allowing Bobby anywhere near the scene?

"Hey, Jablonsky. Miss me already?"

"Yeah." Jablonsky snorted. "I just got some info about the last murder victim. His name was Phillip Cochran and, from what my connections tell me, he was a street hustler. No one really knew who his tricks were, but he seemed to have a lot of money at times and the last two years, he didn't have to go looking for customers. They think he got a reliable gig with someone or some group."

"So our society is hiring street hustlers to become their regulars," he muttered. "Now someone is killing their toys. I wonder how that makes those creeps feel."

"Don't think I really care how a bunch of sickos feel about their boys dying. I just want to stop any more from being drained."

"I'm with you there, buddy." He sighed. "I'm going home. I'll call you when the sun rises in about four hours. I have some licence plates I need you to run for me."

"It's Saturday. Do you really think I want to be in the office running shit for you?"

"You'll be in there, going over the files from this last murder."

"You know me well. Fine, call me and give me those plates. I'll get them turned in. We won't know anything until Monday."

"Great. I'm taking Nik to the track later today. Talk to you soon." He punched the end button on his phone and set it in the console.

When he got home, he stripped and climbed back into bed with Nik. His lover cuddled close as he wrapped his arms around Nik's warm body.

"You okay?" Nik nuzzled Bobby's neck.

"Yeah. I'll be fine. Just need some sleep," he muttered, hoping he could fall back to sleep.

Nik kissed his chest. "Okay. I'll ask you about it all later."

"Thank you, love."

* * * *

"It's another great day to head to the track." Bobby grinned over at Nik as they drove through New York traffic.

"You think any day is a good day to go watch the horses," Nik teased.

He pursed his lips as he pretended to think about what Nik said. Bobby winked. "You're right. Watching something that beautiful doing what it loves and was born to do. It doesn't get any better than that."

His phone rang.

"I should have left the damn thing home," he mumbled as he grabbed it. "Marks."

"Detective Marks, this is Commissioner Lawler."

Bobby pulled the phone away from his ear and stared at it for a moment in surprise. "Sir?"

"Glad I caught you. I wanted to talk to you about the Vanderlist and Thompson cases."

"Ummm…okay, sir. Can I have your address, and I'll be there in a little bit? I have something important to tell you as well."

"Really?"

"Yes, sir."

There was something in the tone of Lawler's voice that made Bobby frown. He repeated the address the commissioner gave him, and Nik wrote it down.

"I'll be there in a few minutes."

"Good." Lawler hung up.

"Who was that?" Nik asked as Bobby turned.

"That was Commissioner Lawler. He wants to talk to me about the case."

"Oh." Disappointment coloured Nik's words.

"Don't worry. I'm sure it won't take long and, maybe by telling him that Vanderlist couldn't have killed those two kids, I'll be able to get back on the case."

Nik didn't reply, just settled back in his seat as Bobby drove them to the commissioner's house. Bobby parked on the street, not wanting to block Lawler's driveway. He kissed Nik quickly before getting out of the car.

"I'll be back in a few minutes."

"I'll be here."

Knocking on the door, Bobby tried not to wonder how much money the commissioner made or if he had family money because his house was a mansion. Lawler opened the door and gestured for Bobby to come in.

"I hope your family doesn't mind you working during the weekend, sir."

Bobby could convey respect, even if he didn't necessarily feel it for the commissioner.

"Oh, my wife and kids went out to our country house for the weekend. One of the girls has a horse show or something." Lawler led the way back to a study.

"What did you want to tell me?" Lawler didn't waste time.

"I've been following Vanderlist around."

"I had Lieutenant O'Donnell take you off the case." Lawler scowled.

"She did, sir. I've been doing it on my own time. Reinholt Vanderlist couldn't have murdered those boys because I have pictures of him dining with two senators and a city councilman at the time the boys were killed."

Bobby hadn't been happy to discover that. He really thought Vanderlist was his best suspect.

"Truly? Pictures?"

"Yes, sir." Bobby pulled out his log book which he'd stuck in his pocket when he got out of his car. Flipping through the pages, he found the notes he wrote for the day the M.E. said the last two victims were killed. "Mr. Vanderlist met Senator Baxter, Senator Chatworth, and Councilman Edwards at the Algonquin from five-thirty to around nine that night. I have pictures of them together."

"I'd like to see these pictures you have." Lawler rested his hip on his desk and pulled a flask out of his pocket.

"I don't have them with me."

Okay, so he was lying. The folder with the photos was in the car with Nik, but every instinct Bobby had screamed not to give up those pictures. It wasn't that he couldn't make more copies or anything like that. Digital cameras had a lot of advantages over film. There was something in Lawler's eyes that made Bobby nervous.

"I expect you to send them to me by the end of the day." Lawler took a sip from the flask without offering Bobby anything. The seal on the flask drew Bobby's gaze.

Before Bobby could answer, his phone rang.

"Marks."

"It's me. You're not going to believe what I've discovered."

* * * *

Alone, Nik picked up the file of photos. He'd gone over them with Bobby earlier, but figured it couldn't hurt to make sure they'd logged everything. He glanced around to make sure Bobby was out of sight and put his feet up on the dash. He giggled at himself, feeling like a naughty kid.

Nik settled in to flip through the pictures one by one. Vanderlist was a handsome man, too bad he was also a pervert. He shook his head at a close-up photo Bobby had taken of Vanderlist's ass as the man walked into an old building. If he hadn't been so secure in his relationship with the hot detective, he might've been jealous.

He set the picture aside, doubting Bobby wanted others to know he'd taken such a shot of one of the wealthiest men in the city. Nik compared the photos against the list of licence plates carefully. The implication of having a car in one of the pictures was too important to screw up a digit.

After checking the list several times, he put the pictures back into the folder with the sheet of paper and stuffed them back into Bobby's briefcase. He glanced at his watch and groaned. "Well, that took ten minutes. Now what?"

Nik had never been good at being idle. He glanced around the Camaro looking for something else to do.

Leave it to Bobby to have probably the cleanest car he'd ever been in.

Bored, he opened the door and unfolded his legs from the dashboard, swinging them to the sidewalk. He doubted he'd need to worry about the city's crime element in Lawler's neighbourhood.

He shook his head as he walked along the sidewalk in front of the commissioner's home. Not a crack, not a crumble. *Rich bastards.*

Even Lawler's driveway was immaculate. Nik stared at the pristine house and grounds. The dark blue convertible at the end of the driveway caught his eye. *Seriously?* Who the hell has a convertible like that in New York? How incredibly unpractical could a person be?

He knew nothing about the commissioner, yet he was disgusted by the man. As he walked back to the Camaro, he started to think about everything Lawler could do with the money he'd spent on the frivolous car that was nothing more than a dick extension in Nik's opinion.

Sliding into the passenger seat, his gaze went to the ass shot of Vanderlist once more. What was Bobby thinking when he took that one?

A splash of blue in the photo had Nik picking it up to examine it closer. "Fuck!"

He scrambled for his new phone and punched in Bobby's number.

"Marks."

"It's me. You're not going to believe what I've discovered."

"Go on."

"I was going through the pictures you took of Vanderlist. I happened to notice the one you took with a close-up of Vanderlist's ass."

"Is that why you're calling?" Bobby questioned.

Nik rolled his eyes. "No. The car just off to the right in the picture is Lawler's. I'm almost positive."

There was a pause on Bobby's end.

"Bobby?"

"Maybe you should make a phone call."

"Jablonsky?"

"Yeah."

"What if we're wrong? It could mean your career."

When once again, there seemed to be a long pause on the other end of the conversation, Nik shifted in the seat. "Bobby?"

Nothing.

"Bobby? Are you there?" Nik pulled the phone away from his ear and looked at the display. "Shit!" They'd been disconnected.

He hit redial, but the call went straight to voicemail. With shaking hands, Nik found Jablonsky's number in his phone. Thank God Bobby had programmed it in as soon as they'd purchased the new cell.

As he waited for the detective to pick up, he climbed out of the car.

"Jablonsky."

"It's Nik. We're at the commissioner's house. Bobby's inside and I found something that points to Lawler as the killer. I called Bobby and now nothing," he fired off.

"Hold it. Slow down. Why're you at Lawlers?"

"I don't know. He said he needed to speak to Bobby. Please, you've got to help him." Nik paced in front of the house, not sure if he should burst in and save the day, or do the smart thing and wait for Jablonsky.

"I'm on my way. It'll take me a while to get there though."

"Shit!" Nik scrambled to hide in the bushes as he spotted Bobby and Lawler coming out of the house. "I don't think Bobby has a while. Lawler's leading him to his car at gunpoint."

Nik's breathing picked up as he struggled with what to do. He knew he should probably rush the commissioner. Maybe that would at least buy Bobby some time to overpower Lawler? Or maybe it would get his lover shot.

"Stay where you are. Don't even think about it," Jablonsky growled into the phone.

"What? How'd you…"

"Because I'd be tempted to do the same thing, but you're unarmed and untrained."

"Well then what the hell am I supposed to do? I can't hide here and let Lawler drive away with Bobby. We'll never find them again."

"You've got Bobby's car, right?"

"Yeah."

"Follow them."

Nik swallowed around a large lump in his throat as the Jaguar pulled out of the driveway with Bobby at the wheel.

"I don't drive," he finally admitted. "And they're getting away."

"Dammit! I'm still too far out to catch up with them. You'll have to do your best, Nik."

Do my best. Right. Nik jumped from out of the bushes and ran to the Camaro. He got behind the wheel and searched around for a way to pull the seat up. "I'm putting you on speaker. This is gonna take all the concentration I have."

"Just remember to shout out streets and directions as you go."

Nik started the powerful engine. As he put the car into drive, he tried to calm his breathing. He wouldn't do Bobby any good if he freaked out before even catching up to him. The car lurched out of its parking spot and Nik headed it towards the spec of blue in the distance.

Shit, shit, shit. He almost panicked when he had to pass his first oncoming car. *Stay on your own side of the street, Nik.*

"Directions, Nik!"

"Uhh, east. Coming up on Fifth Avenue. Please don't turn left." The blue Jag turned left as feared. "Oh fuck, why does he have to go up Fifth Avenue?"

"You're doing fine, Nik. Calm down."

Nik shrieked as a cab nearly sideswiped Bobby's car. "People are crazy!"

He did his best to keep the Jaguar in his sights. "I think Bobby knows I'm back here. He's not driving in his usual reckless manner."

"Good."

"He's turning east again." Nik gave Jablonsky the street. "Oh fuck, I almost hit someone."

Tears started to burn at Nik's eyes as he realised how much damage he could do. The blurred vision didn't help matters as he sideswiped a parked car, taking off the Camaro's passenger-side mirror.

"What the hell was that?"

"Bobby's gonna kill me."

"Can you still drive?"

"Yeah." He wanted to scream no. He wanted to beg Jablonsky to find him and take him to the man he loved. He wanted a hell of a lot. The reality was that he was the only person standing between Bobby and a killer.

"We're crossing over to Queens."

"I'm gaining ground, Nik. I'm about five minutes behind you."

"Well, catch the fuck up and let me out of this car!"

He heard Jablonsky chuckle, which pissed Nik off further. He knew he sounded like a whiney candy-ass, but with every red light, every passing car, he knew he was riding the edge of killing himself or someone else.

A car came out of nowhere and clipped the front of the Camaro, sending the vehicle into a spin. Nik's life flashed before his eyes before he could get the Camaro stopped.

The man in the other vehicle stopped and started to get out of his car. Nik held up a hand and turned the Camaro back in the direction the Jaguar was heading. He could hear something rubbing against the front tire. "And they say public transportation is dangerous."

Nik doubted he'd ever get into another car as long as he lived. He shouted more directions to Jablonsky. "Wait a minute. He's slowing down in front of a row of buildings."

"Pull over. Now. You don't want Lawler to spot you."

"Yeah, yeah, yeah." Nik pulled to the kerb and shut off the engine. "I'm about two blocks away. They're getting out of the car. There's an old, faded sign over the building that says Fontelli's Fresh Fruit."

"Got it. You stick tight, and I'll be there in…crap! There's some sort of traffic jam. I'll try to go around."

Nik watched as Lawler handed Bobby the keys to the building. Bobby glanced down the street in Nik's direction and gave a slight shake of his head. Bobby unlocked the door, but instead of opening it, he swung around with the keys still in hand.

Nik gasped as Lawler's head flew to the side, bringing the gun up to slam against the side of Bobby's head. Nik watched horrified as Bobby started to sag towards the pavement. Lawler pushed Bobby inside the building as Nik sat stunned.

"I've got to help him." As he jumped out of the car, he heard Jablonsky yelling at him, but he didn't care.

Chapter Fourteen

Bobby's head rang, and his feet weren't obeying his mind. God, who knew Lawler would slug him with his gun? Should have thought about that before he tried to make his move.

Nik. The thought of his lover following him scared Bobby. It had nothing to do with the fact Nik couldn't drive, and he'd have to take Bobby's beloved car. What worried Bobby the most was simply that Nik would try to save him, and Lawler would shoot him.

"Let's go. You brought this all on yourself, Marks. If you had just kept your nose out of it all, I wouldn't have to do this." Lawler shook his head.

"I'm a good detective. It's my job to solve murders. Maybe you should have gotten rid of the bodies in a way that was different from your friend Thompson."

"Show some respect when you talk to me." Lawler slapped Bobby across the face.

Blinking away the stars, he shook his head. "Respect? You get your jollies playing with boys? That's sick. Sorry, but perverts don't garner much respect from me."

"You don't understand."

Lawler pushed him down a corridor, keeping him moving with nudges in the middle of his back from his gun. He grimaced as Lawler managed to hit him hard in the kidneys.

"Bastard."

He tripped into a room when Lawler jerked him to the right. Lights burned his eyes and he closed them, trying to adjust to the sudden brightness.

"Open your eyes."

Another smack to his head had him swinging and a sick satisfaction burned through him when he heard the gasp and the thud of his fist hitting flesh.

"Don't hit me again."

A fist drove into his stomach, doubling him over. His face hit a knee and he went to the floor, catching himself at the last minute with his hands. Staring down, Bobby noticed the drops of blood that coloured the grey concrete dark red. *Fuck.* His damn nose was broken again and he'd have at least one, if not two, black eyes when this was all said and done. Unless Lawler shot him. Of course, he'd rather be shot than have his throat slashed and drained of blood.

Pain burned through him as Lawler grabbed his hair and jerked his head back. He stared up into the man's feverish eyes.

"Get up."

Bobby struggled to his feet—doing his best to push the pain away—and looked around. Shock hit him. It was the same kind of room that Thompson had in his house. A bed held the prominent position in the middle of the room like an altar. An armoire sat against one wall. Bobby didn't want to think about what was in that cabinet.

Lawler shoved him towards a chair placed to the side of the bed. "Sit."

"I'm not a dog."

"You are whatever I say you are." Pushing him into the chair, Lawler tossed him a pair of handcuffs. "Handcuff yourself to the chair."

Snapping the cuffs around his wrist, Bobby got his right hand hooked to the arm of the chair. When that was done, Lawler came closer and captured Bobby's left wrist. Bobby tugged, testing the cuffs and realised he wasn't going anywhere at the moment. He hoped Nik had called Jablonsky, and his partner was already figuring out a way to get him out of there. Bobby really hoped Nik stayed outside and didn't attempt to save him.

Nik didn't have the training to keep from getting shot by Lawler. While Bobby didn't think the commissioner was interested in drinking his blood, his gut told him things might change if Lawler caught a glimpse of Nik.

"Why did you kill them?"

"Who?" Lawler glanced around, searching for something.

"Mavis Vanderlist, Phillip Cochran, and those two other boys." Anger surged in him as he came to the conclusion Lawler didn't remember the names of his victims.

"I needed their blood. Mavis wasn't my first choice, but I wasn't able to find one of my regular whores. They were being used by the others."

Bobby watched Lawler pull a flask out of his pocket and sip from it. "What's that?"

Lawler glanced down at the object in his hand. "It's a family heirloom."

He held it up for Bobby to study. Bobby grimaced when he recognised the seal on the flask's front.

"So being a sick bastard runs in the family, huh? Did your father abuse you? Do you abuse your son?"

He didn't flinch at the backhand slap Lawler levelled at him.

"I would never touch my own son and my father didn't touch me that way. He did teach me the sublime and life-altering experiences one can achieve when loving a younger man. The Knights of Pederastia isn't a group of perverted old men taking advantage of innocent children."

Bobby couldn't keep his snort of disbelief from breaking through.

"You're a heathen. You wouldn't understand how spiritual such a union can be. If it were up to me, everyone would know the love and true spirituality that comes from entering the innocent." Lawler took another sip from the flask as he knelt in front of a chest at the foot of the bed and opened it.

"What are you drinking?"

"Thompson didn't understand what he'd gotten when he bought that cask of wine. He just knew it was from Radu cel Frumos, the Ruler of our society. The fool never grasped what the wine could do to a man."

Lawler pulled out a cask exactly like the one Bobby found at Thompson's house. The way the commissioner handled it told Bobby, Lawler knew what he held in his hands. Not just the historical value of the actual object, but the importance of the liquid inside.

"Drinking it too fast caused it to go to his head. If he planned on using it, he should have sipped it. The only way to control the beast within is to keep him on a leash."

"The beast?"

A faint noise caught Bobby's ear and he gritted his teeth, hoping against hope that it was Jablonsky and SWAT, not Nik, coming to save him. Lawler didn't react to the sound.

"Yes. I'm sure you've heard of Vlad Dracul."

"Dracula? Sure, I've read the book and everything."

Sarcasm seemed lost on Lawler.

"Bram Stoker's book exaggerated the true nature of what Vlad was. He was a usurper and murderer, but the wine made him stronger. It made him more cunning. He was the true trainer of the beast."

"What the fuck is this beast you keep talking about?"

"The beast will give a man power and wealth beyond his wildest dreams as long as he continues to feed him."

"Really? And how'd that work out for Vlad, because I'm pretty sure he's nothing but ashes by now."

The vague wave of Lawler's hand told Bobby he discounted those issues.

"Vlad ran out of wine. I believe a servant stole the other bottles and deserted Vlad. You don't get it though. Radu made this wine. It's his soul that touched it and imbued the drink with the power of the Knights." Lawler stroked the cask lovingly.

"Radu used the blood and heart of his brother and father to create that wine. He used his own blood to call forth the demon to anoint the wine."

Scrapes came from the corridor and Bobby braced his feet against the floor, pushing his chair across the concrete, trying to cover whoever was coming down the hall.

Lawler shot a frown over his shoulder at Bobby, but immediately went back to staring at the cask.

Bobby had to keep Lawler's attention away from whoever was coming. He decided to use the time left to get a few more answers out of the madman. "What does Professor Lattimer have to do with this?"

"Lattimer?" Lawler snorted. "He fancies himself the archivist of The Knights of Paiderastia. Hack is what he is. Your little boyfriend found more of our artefacts than Lattimer did."

"Why did you kill all those people? Was it just for their blood?"

"No. Mavis tried to blackmail me. She had figured out what 'club' her father and I belonged to. She was disgusted, but she wasn't going to her father to get the money. She came to me and threatened to tell my wife if I didn't give her hundreds of thousands of dollars." He shook his head. "The beast needed to be fed anyway, so I figured why not let him have his way with her."

"And you didn't want your wife to know. Why didn't you just pay her?"

"It's my wife's money. I married a woman whose family is worth millions. Either way, I would have had to tell her, and I won't jeopardise my chances at governor by pissing off my wife or the men in the society with me."

"I don't think you need to worry about those men," Bobby confessed.

Lawler whirled towards him and he was glad that he faced the door, so whoever was coming up the corridor wouldn't be seen by Lawler.

"What are you talking about?"

Bobby shrugged. "We got a list from the auctioneer of men who were invited to bid on the casks. We know all of those men are members of your pathetic little club. The police will be going after them, once we've taken care of you."

"Taken care of me?" Lawler laughed. "How are you going to do that? No one knows where you are."

"You never know about that. Why did you kill Phillip and the other kids?"

"Phillip panicked when he saw you. He wanted money to leave."

"Instead of just giving it to him and letting him disappear, you slit his throat and drank his blood. After you ruined his life, you took it from him as well."

The commissioner's puzzled expression caught Bobby off-guard.

"Ruined his life? How did I do that? He was already selling himself on the street when we found him. We took him under our wing and gave him a better life. He would have been dead long before I ended his life."

"A better life? Being the plaything to a bunch of disgusting old men? I'm sure you think he should have been grateful that you let him live as long as he did."

"I took his blood because, unlike Mavis, he was untainted by drugs and alcohol. Pure blood is marvellous and intoxicating."

Bobby swallowed hard, not wanting to vomit all over himself while he was captive. Well, unless he could projectile it all over the commissioner. The bastard deserved to be covered in puke as far as Bobby was concerned.

"The other two were the same. You don't understand how powerful blood can make you. How strong and invincible you are with it coursing through your veins."

That feverish look built in Lawler's eyes and Bobby realised the wine was starting to kick in. God, he hoped Jablonsky and the others showed up before Lawler decided that drinking Bobby's blood wouldn't be that bad.

It certainly wasn't pure, considering all the alcohol he'd consumed over the years, but still, blood was blood.

A head peeked around the frame of the door and Bobby almost groaned in fear. Fuck, it was Nik. He thought his lover was smart enough not to come inside and to wait for Jablonsky. He shook his head. Bobby should have known Nik wouldn't wait, but why did his lover's brave streak have to show up now?

"Why did you dump Phillip in the alley behind the club?"

"I knew you were interested in Vanderlist. By putting clues in places that would draw your eye to him, I could ensure you wouldn't look my way." Lawler chuckled. "Of course, I didn't realise you were actually following the man. Your lieutenant never told me that."

"She didn't know." He kept track of Nik out of the corner of his eye. Bobby didn't want to do anything that would alert Lawler to Nik's presence. "I followed Vanderlist on my own. I knew there was something I was missing. I just couldn't figure out what."

"It was the last two bodies that gave me away. I should've made sure I knew where Vanderlist was before I killed them. But they looked so enticing, and I could hear their blood rushing through their veins." The commissioner nodded to the bed in the middle of the room. "I killed them right there. The look in their eyes was priceless when they realised what I was doing. I cut their throats and drank from their jugulars while they bled out. Fresh blood is more exhilarating than the most expensive wine."

* * * *

Nik listened at the door as Bobby tried to keep Lawler talking. Upon entering the building, he'd found a thin metal pipe. Nik doubted the weight would do much good, but something was better than nothing. If he was lucky, he could distract the commissioner long enough for Bobby to get free.

As he peered into the pervert's lair, he noticed the handcuffs on Bobby's wrists. *Shit.* Simply distracting Lawler was no longer an option. He glanced over his shoulder. Where the hell was Jablonsky?

Nik decided to hold his position until either his backup arrived or he sensed an imminent threat directed Bobby's way. He knew Bobby was aware of his presence. If nothing else, his lover knew he wasn't alone.

"What do you hope to gain by drinking the wine? I mean, is it a high for you to kill innocent people?" Bobby asked Lawler.

"A high?" Lawler seemed to think about the question.

Nik could tell the commissioner was having a hard time concentrating by the expression on the man's face.

"It's so much greater than a high. It's the closest thing to total self-awareness I've found. To free yourself of all inhibitions. To finally reach the place where you're in complete control of those around you." Lawler shook his head. "Who needs a God in heaven when you feel like a god on earth? I am that god, and soon the entire city will bow before me."

"You're fucking insane," Bobby spat.

Lawler smiled. "Perhaps, but the same could be said about the most powerful men in history."

"So what are your plans for me?" Bobby asked.

"You?" Lawler laughed. "There's a very special meeting being held here this evening. I will show The Knights my power by taking down a member of law enforcement. It will prove to them no one is beyond my reach. I'd originally planned a little show for my brothers involving one of the boys in our stable, but this will be so much better. I only wish there had been time to summon The Ruler."

A noise drew Nik's attention. He gestured Jablonsky over. Guns made him nervous, but he almost dropped to his knees in thanks as he spotted the one in Jablonsky's hand.

Inside the room, Lawler had begun pulling items out of the large armoire and laying them on the bed. The midnight blue hooded satin robe made Nik nervous, but not nearly as much as the white one Lawler held up in front of Bobby.

"I can't imagine anything more beautiful than the crimson of your blood against the purity of this robe." Lawler was gleeful in his ramblings.

"I'm going to unlock one of your cuffs, but don't try anything stupid." Lawler pulled a set of keys from his pocket and walked towards Bobby, gun in hand.

Nik glanced over his shoulder at Jablonsky. He knew it was the perfect time for a rescue attempt. Jablonsky nodded and Nik stepped to the side.

Unable to see into the room from his position, Nik closed his eyes and hoped for the best.

"Lawler!" Jablonsky yelled. "You're under arrest. Put the gun down. Put the gun down! Now!"

Nik flinched as two shots rang out. He covered his face with his shaking hands as he waited for a sound from Bobby.

"Call 9-1-1," Jablonsky ordered from the doorway.

"Bobby?"

He could tell by the expression on Jablonsky's face it wasn't good. "He's down."

Heedless of the potential danger, Nik pushed past Jablonsky and burst into the room. Lawler lay to the left of Bobby with a gunshot wound to the chest, but he didn't care. He dropped the useless pipe he'd been holding.

"Bobby?" He fell to his knees in front of the man he loved. Bobby's head lagged forward and Nik started to tilt it up.

"Don't!" Jablonsky shouted. "He's been shot in the neck."

Nik's hand smoothed down the sides of Bobby's neck. "Get these cuffs off him!"

On the phone, Jablonsky moved forward and found the keys where they'd fallen to the floor.

"Bobby, honey? Wake up." His hand past over a slight indention. Taking off his own shirt, Nik held it to the wound. "I don't think it's as bad as it looks."

Bobby made a groaning sound, giving Nik hope. "Bobby?"

"What…"

"Shhh, don't talk. An ambulance is on the way."

"Lawler…"

"He's dead," Jablonsky answered, unlocking the remaining handcuff.

"Did you see it?" With his hands free, Bobby fell forwards out of the chair and against Nik's chest. The weight of the much bigger man felt like heaven to Nik. He continued to press his, once yellow, shirt against Bobby's wound.

The smell of blood threatened to overwhelm him, but he held himself together for Bobby's sake. "I love you," he whispered to the man in his arms.

"Love you," Bobby grit out between clenched teeth.

Nik heard the sirens first. "They're here." Without taking his eyes off Bobby, he addressed Jablonsky. "Go get them. Tell them to hurry."

Jablonsky ran from the room.

He gave Bobby the best smile he could muster. "It's going to be okay. You just stay awake for me."

"If I don't make it…"

"None of that," Nik said, cutting Bobby off.

"There's a meeting here. Tell Jablonsky."

"I will."

Jablonsky burst back into the room with several policemen and E.M.T.s. Jablonsky held Nik by the shoulders as the emergency personnel started to work on Bobby. "He's going to be fine."

Nik turned and buried his face against Jablonsky's chest. "I can't lose him."

Jablonsky seemed to hesitate for a few moments before wrapping his arms around Nik. "You won't. Bobby's a tough son-of-a-bitch."

Epilogue

Hanging up the phone, Bobby glared at it for a minute until Nik spoke.

"So what did the garage say?"

The tentative tone of Nik's voice caught his attention. He turned to look at his lover, poised nervously at the entrance of the living room. Strolling across the room, he encircled Nik's waist and dragged the slender man tight to him.

"It'll be another month before the damn Camaro's fixed." He grumbled, not happy about being left without transportation. "It's already been a month. There wasn't that much damage."

"I'm sorry."

It was, like, the thousandth time Nik apologised for wrecking Bobby's car.

"Ah, stop saying you're sorry, honey. I'd rather it be totalled than you being hurt or killed in it." He nuzzled the little triangular area at the base of Nik's throat. "It's just a car. Not nearly as important to me as you are."

"But it's your dream car," Nik protested, but his voice softened as Bobby licked a line along his jugular.

"Sure, it was my dream car and made me happy for a while, but not nearly as happy as you're going to make me for the rest of our lives." Bobby bent and started to sweep Nik up into his arms.

"Wait." Nik placed his hands on Bobby's chest and pushed him away a few inches. "No lifting me. The doctors might have cleared you to go back to work on Monday, but they still don't want you straining that wound until it's completely healed."

He frowned, but didn't argue. Nik had been like a mother hen while he recuperated from the gunshot wound Lawler gave him. Bobby couldn't help being thrilled when he'd heard that Jablonsky killed Lawler. The man deserved worse than being shot for everything he'd done. He'd tried on several occasions to explain the flash of light he'd witnessed as Lawler was shot, but Nik and the doctors kept telling him it was because he'd also just been shot. The more he thought about the things Lawler said about the beast within, the more he questioned what he saw in that last second before the man died.

"Stop that." Nik patted him on the cheek.

"What?"

"No thinking about Lawler. Not when we were about to move this show into the bedroom."

He winked, even while he tried to be serious. "Are you sure I was going to the bedroom? Maybe I was going to bend you over the couch and fuck that pretty little ass right there."

Nik swallowed and he couldn't seem to make his tongue work anymore. Bobby took pity on his lover, grabbed his hand, and dragged him down the hall to their bedroom.

During the time he recovered from his injuries, he spent the majority of his off time at Nik's house. Nik fussed a lot over his bandages and making sure Bobby wasn't over exerting himself, but as much as he grumbled about it, it was nice having someone take care of him like that.

Pushing open the door, he gestured to the bed. "Get naked and on the bed."

A laugh threatened to burst from his mouth at the speed Nik showed getting undressed and spread eagle on the bed. All Bobby could think was thank God they kept the lube close because he didn't want to take the time to search for it.

"Touch yourself," he ordered while unbuttoning his shirt.

Wicked was the only word Bobby could use to describe the expression on Nik's face as his lover licked his own fingers and reached down to circle around his hole.

"Shit." His shirt hit the floor with his jeans and underwear following close behind.

"You weren't specific about what I was to touch." Nik closed his eyes with a blissful sigh as his fingers sank into his ass.

Bobby climbed onto the bed, crawling over to where Nik's thighs sprawled and his fingers moved in and out of his hole. Bobby pressed his own finger in with Nik's, stretching his lover. Soon four fingers teased and played, driving Bobby crazy as Nik lifted his hips.

The wet crown of Nik's cock brushed against Bobby's chin. Arranging his head, Bobby opened his mouth and took Nik in, sucking hard with each thrust.

"Oh God." Nik groaned. "Bobby, in me now."

Bobby wasn't about to disobey that command. He came off Nik's cock with a slurp and gestured with his free hand towards the pillows.

"Lube."

Nik dug under the pillows and covers, searching for the tube while Bobby continued to rub against Nik's gland with his knuckles as he waited.

"Here."

He ducked Nik's flailing hand to grab the slick before Nik hit him with it. "Thanks."

"Please," Nik pleaded with his voice and every inch of his body.

Bobby's cock was hard enough to pound Nik through the mattress. He shuddered as he smeared the lube over his length. He tossed the tube over his shoulder, not caring where it ended up.

Kneeling between Nik's thighs, Bobby positioned his cock at Nik's entrance and pushed forward, an explosive moan ripping from him as he buried himself balls deep in Nik's channel.

"Damn." Bobby bowed his head, resting it on Nik's shoulder for a moment as he regained his control. He hoped for a little more finesse than to go at Nik like a moose during mating season.

Nik ran his hands up and down Bobby's back, undulating, slightly encouraging Bobby to move. "Are you all right? You didn't hurt yourself?"

"No, love. Sometimes making love to you is like coming home and it takes my breath away."

Nik inhaled sharply and Bobby glanced at him, surprised to see tears in those dark green eyes of his.

"What did I say?"

"Nothing really." Nik jerked Bobby's head down and crushed their lips together in a quick kiss before letting him go with a slap to his ass. "Get moving, buddy. I'm aching to come."

"So am I."

Bobby hooked Nik's legs over his arms and started pounding Nik's ass. The salty scent of sweat and sex filled the air along with the steady slap of skin on skin. Nik braced one hand against the headboard to keep from banging his head into it. The other he wrapped around his cock, pumping in rhythm with Bobby's thrusts.

Harsh panting echoed through the room. Pressure built along Bobby's spine, pooling at the base and drawing his balls tight to his body.

"Nik," he warned.

Nik clenched his inner passage around Bobby's cock, milking him as Bobby's climax broke.

"Fuck," Bobby shouted, buried his dick as deep inside Nik as he could and froze, flooding Nik's ass with his cum.

"God!"

Nik's cum painted his stomach and hands while Bobby shuddered and collapsed on top of Nik.

"Ompf."

"Sorry."

Bobby rolled to the side, keeping a hand on Nik's chest. Their heartbeats slowed and evened out as their breathing calmed as well. Grinning, Bobby stared up at the ceiling. After a few minutes, Nik climbed out of bed and went to the bathroom. When he came back, he cleaned Bobby off before tossing the washcloth into a laundry basket nearby.

They slipped under the blankets and snuggled close. It seemed like a good time for a nap. Nik had other ideas.

"Did you talk to Jablonsky earlier today?"

"Yes." Bobby rolled onto his side and braced his head on his hand to look down at Nik. "Why?"

"Did he say anything about Professor Lattimer or the society?"

"Lattimer's still missing. They've completed the search of his house, but there's nothing. Not so much as a scrap of paper to indicate where he's gone."

"And the others?"

"I didn't tell you this before?" He frowned as he thought about what his partner had told him earlier. "Jablonsky got pictures and names of all the men who showed up for that meeting. They'll keep the society's members under surveillance. If they do anything wrong, we'll be there to snap their asses up."

"Why can't you arrest them now?" Nik sounded indignant. "They hurt young boys. They had a hand in killing those people."

"No, they didn't. Lawler killed four of them and Thompson killed the others. We have no proof they did anything to that stable of boys Lawler talked about. It's terrible and horrible for those boys, but it's an unfortunate fact of our justice system. We can't arrest them on rumour." Bobby traced Nik's ribs.

"That's not fair."

Bobby brushed a kiss over Nik's cheek. "I know that, love, but it's a fact of life. We'll do what we can to catch them doing something illegal and put them in jail. Trust me. Guys like that don't change their stripes."

"I just…"

He pressed a finger to Nik's lips. "Let's talk about something else. Who is going to move in with whom?"

"What?" Surprise raced across Nik's face.

"You weren't expecting that? Hell, Nik, I've practically lived here since I was shot. It makes sense to live together. I plan on spending a great deal of time with you, and I hate sleeping by myself. Why keep two places? We can combine our stuff."

Nik seemed to think about it, and Bobby drummed his fingers on Nik's stomach.

Finally, he couldn't take it anymore. "What the hell is there to think about?"

Nik rocketed into Bobby's arms and covered his face with kisses. "Hell yeah, I'll move in with you. Actually, I think you should move in with me since I own this house and you rent. You probably don't have as much stuff as I do either. And my house is closer to the university."

"Shit. That means I have to ride the damn subway into the precinct until my car's ready." Bobby frowned.

"Oh, we can wait until your car is ready. That way you wouldn't have to take the bus or anything." Nik looked disappointed at the thought of Bobby not moving in right away.

"Sweetheart, I'd take the subway all the way to Albany if it meant I could sleep with you every night." He kissed Nik. "I'll call Jablonsky and see when I can get him to help me move."

He cuddled Nik close and sighed. God, he adored the feeling of Nik next to him and it looked like he would get to have the man he loved forever.

"I love you," he whispered in Nik's ear.

"I love you as well, Detective Marks. Who would have thought wine meant for Vlad Dracul could bring two such different people together?"

"Yeah. The world's weird like that."

He closed his eyes and synced his breathing with Nik until they both drifted off to sleep.

* * * *

"A package from the United States has arrived for you, Sir."

"Thank you, Steven. Have it taken to my office."

"Yes, Sir."

He smiled at the thought of the long awaited crate. Pity he'd had to go all the way to America to buy something that had originally come from the region he lived in. Jules Worthington finished off his coffee and strode through to his office.

As expected, the shipping crate sat on a protective pad on top of his hundred-year old French Gothic desk. A small, manageable, crowbar sat next to the invaluable wooden box. "Excellent."

Jules turned back to his secretary, sitting just outside the office. "Hold my calls, Steven. I do not wish to be disturbed."

"Yes, Sir."

Jules locked his office door and circled his desk several times, eyeing the crate. If the research they'd spent millions of dollars to obtain was correct, the contents of the unobtrusive wooden box would change the face of history.

Standing behind his desk, he picked up the crowbar and carefully began removing the top of the crate. With a squeal of protest, the last nail fell to the padding below. Jules set down the crowbar and lifted the lid to peer inside. He was perturbed by all the packaging material, but finally dug his way to his prize.

"There you are, my lovely. We've got great plans for you."

Jules reached for the phone and punched in the prearranged number. As he waited, he couldn't resist running a hand over the aged pottery.

"Yes."

"It's here," Jules announced, pulling his hand back as if the person on the other end of the phone would catch his indiscretion.

"Good. You know what to do."

"Yes, Your Majesty. I'll take care of it."

About the Authors

Carol Lynne

An avid reader for years, one day Carol Lynne decided to write her own brand of erotic romance. Carol juggles between being a full-time mother and a full-time writer. These days, you can usually find Carol either cleaning jelly out of the carpet or nestled in her favourite chair writing steamy love scenes.

T.A. Chase

There is beauty in every kind of love, so why not live a life without boundaries? Experiencing everything the world offers fascinates TA and writing about the things that make each of us unique is how TA shares those insights. TA lives in the Midwest with a wonderful partner of twelve years. When not writing, TA's watching movies, reading and living life to the fullest.

Carol Lynne and T.A. Chase love to hear from readers. You can find their contact information, website details and author profile page at http://www.total-e-bound.com.

Total-E-Bound Publishing

www.total-e-bound.com

Take a look at our exciting range of literagasmic™
erotic romance titles and discover pure quality
at Total-E-Bound.